D1389700

PAPER BUTTERFLY

PAPER BUTTERFLY

DIANE WEI LIANG

PICADOR

First published 2007 in Picador by Pan Macmillan Australia Pty Limited, Sydney

First published in Great Britain 2008 by Picador
an imprint of Pan Macmillan Ltd
Pan Macmillan, 20 New Wharf Road, London N1 9RR
Basingstoke and Oxford
Associated companies throughout the world
www.panmacmillan.com

ISBN 978-0-330-44776-8 HB
ISBN 978-0-330-45609-8 TPB

1 3 5 7 9 8 6 4 2

A CIP catalogue record for this book is available from
the British Library.

Printed and bound in the UK by
CPI Mackays, Chatham ME5 8TB

www.dianeweiliang.com

Visit **www.picador.com** to read more about all our books
and to buy them. You will also find features, author interviews and
news of any author events, and you can sign up for e-newsletters
so that you're always first to hear about our new releases.

Once again, for my mother

and

for Andreas, Alexander and Elisabeth

Prologue

East Wind Lao Gai Camp
Gansu province, China
December 1989

On they went, singing, "Communism is the red lantern of our
heart" their voices soaring above the bitter wind. Their feet
trampled on dead grass and bare earth. They swung their arms
in rhythm, holding their heads upright, eyes fixed on each
other's shaven heads. They sang eagerly, forcefully. Two words,
lao gai — work and reform — were emblazoned in white on
their padded grey jackets. Behind them, the sky was the colour
of sand, the sun white.

This land offered nothing but harsh wind and dry yellow
earth. Under the dome of the sky, snow-peaked mountains
stood like unwanted burdens of the past. This was the province
where the Great Wall ended, that the Silk Road had passed
through. Both had lain forgotten for the last thousand years.

The guards opened the gate to let the convicts in. Above the high wall five red characters, East Wind Lao Gai Camp, confronted them.

"Halt!"

The prisoners stopped.

"Face forward!"

Officer Grasshopper Yao, tall, coat-hanger shoulders, called the roll. A red star, small but highly polished, shone in the fur of his hat.

"Twelve thirty-one."

"Dao." The prisoner shouted yes.

"Fifty-six thirty-four."

"Dao."

A sudden gust blew sand into the air, as though a truck was unloading on a construction site, and 3424 closed his eyes. He was a young man: the contours of his face were those of a boy, his skin yet to roughen, physique to fill out.

The guard swung his club and the prisoner fell to the ground, blood gushing, his handsome face ruined.

"Answer, Lin, you anti-Party, anti-revolutionary swine!"

"It was the wind, the sand," Lin mumbled, blood trickling through his fingers. He didn't look up. He was trying to discover where the pain was coming from. When he touched the gash on his cheek, he shrieked.

Now the guard kicked his ribs. Lin screamed and crumpled to the ground.

"Silence! You're here to reform yourself!" the guard yelled. "The first thing you will learn is respect. When you're asked a

question, you will answer. If you defy the People, the People will crush you. Do you hear?"

"Yes, sir!" the ranks of prisoners shouted in unison.

East Wind Lao Gai Camp consisted of row upon row of barracks. Convicts, normally in pairs, shared small cells in each block. The blocks had low ceilings, with lightbulbs glaring from cone-shaped shades. The floors were stone, from the local quarry. Each cell contained two bedrolls, two washing basins, two towels and one latrine bucket.

Lin coughed, and tasted blood. Above the gash, his left eye had swollen. His cellmate, Little Soldier, tried to clean the wound, but Lin snatched the towel. "I'll do it," he said. The cut was raw, and he gasped when he touched it.

Little Soldier squatted, as far away from the latrine bucket as he could. "He's making you pay for yesterday. You can't fight Grasshopper Yao."

Lin spat blood. "How long can he keep it up?"

"Till you give up. Just bite your lip and don't rise to him. Then maybe he'll get bored, move on to someone else."

"I'm in here for whatever crime I committed, but he has no right to beat me. I'll protest to the authorities."

"Protest? You won't get anywhere by writing letters. Look at Old Tang. They put him in a little black cell for a year with no light. And what about Cripple? He wasn't a cripple when he came in. The brutes in Number Two made a mess of him. Guards' idea, I heard." Little Soldier chewed his nails. "College kid, do nothing — or you'll get yourself killed. Let it go. You can't change anything."

Dinner came on aluminium plates, the same every day, wotou, or hard corn bun, mixed with vegetables.

"Thirty-four twenty-four, you didn't complete your quota today. Half rations for you." A single wotou, the size of Lin's fist, lay on his plate.

They squatted to eat.

"You must reach your quota, Lin." Little Soldier swallowed. "Your hands are like a girl's, but not for long working in the lime kiln." He showed Lin his hands, which were dark brown and calloused. "These are worker's hands. I do my quota and lie low. Two more years, and then I'll go home to my mama. No more bootlegging. I'll find a woman and be happy."

"Does your ma know where you are?"

"She may. They caught us in Inner Mongolia with our mules. My brother was our leader. They put a bullet in the back of his head. Mama had to pay for the bullet, she said. I haven't seen her since they pushed me onto a truck to come here. They didn't tell me where I was going."

"Have you had letters from her?"

"She can't write. A man in our village writes letters for everyone, but not for my mama."

"I've not heard from Grandpa either. He can't know where I am or he'd write. I don't think anyone knows where I am."

The wotou was hard to chew and even harder to swallow.

"He'll be waiting for you. My mama's waiting for me, I know." Little Soldier thumped his chest.

"Maybe he's dead. He was seventy-two when I was arrested. I think of him every day. I wish I could just send a few lines to him. I don't want him to worry."

"Do nothing — understand?"

"If I ever get out of here, I swear I'll —" Lin clenched his fists.

"Your cut's open again." Little Soldier grabbed the towel and handed it to Lin. "Press it hard."

At night, Lin lay on his bedroll, the stench of the latrine bucket overpowering. Little Soldier snored. Through the tiny window high on the wall, he could see the clear night sky and a star.

He remembered the stars of Beijing's summer nights, the scent of grapes and the cool shade of the vines. Grandpa and he had sat on the doorstep, fanning themselves. It was too hot to sleep. Mosquitoes hung in the air in packs.

Grandpa had told stories: Guan Yin and Liu Hui, the Legend of the Three Kingdoms; the Monkey King and Monk Tangseng; the Saga of the Kong Fu Knights. "They are stories for boys, for you," he had said. "Boys must learn faith and loyalty."

For twenty years, Grandpa had watched him grow. There had been elementary school, fist fights, his first bicycle, the first three-good award, football, catching dragonflies in the city moat, studying late at night. Now the doorstep was worn, the middle bowed.

He had left Grandpa to go to university. Lin had never seen the ocean but he wanted to study oceanography. He had liked the idea of roaming the sea in its infinity. He wanted to learn more of the sea animals he had read about and seen on television in nature programmes. When Lin was at high school, their neighbours, the Chens, had bought a TV set and he had gone next door to watch it whenever a nature programme was showing. He had grown up with the Chens' son, whom everyone called Fatty even after he had grown into a slender young man.

"Go," said Grandpa, sitting cross-legged on his bed. "A good son travels the four seas. Your mother and father would have been proud of you. Don't worry about me. I have strong bones. Besides, I have our neighbours. Nothing will happen to me."

Lin wrote to his grandfather from university. He wrote about the sea that at last he had seen, shimmering under the dawn light. He told his grandfather that he had never seen anything more beautiful. "The sound of the sea, Grandpa," he remembered writing, "is like a song. Some hear it. Some feel it. Many remember it."

It was by the sea that he first saw her, like a song he couldn't forget. Her fair skin, open smile and large brown eyes were as alluring to him as the sea.

The day she said she loved him, he was the happiest man on earth. They were walking on the beach and Venus sparkled in the sky, as if she were sending a secret message to the lovers below. The air tasted salty and they were filled with desire and love. The waves lapped gently on the shore.

Lin woke. His body ached from twelve hours in the lime kiln. The gash on his face felt as if it had been the work of a *hundred knives rather than a club. Her touch vanished. Around his head, the bedroll was damp.*

Deliberately Lin rubbed at his wound until it opened again. He ground his teeth. Remember this pain, this night, and every day of lao gai, *he ordered himself. Remember your enemies. Never forget.*

PART ONE

1

It was two weeks before Chinese New Year, the Spring Festival that marks the end of winter. It is the principal holiday of the year, with celebrations that last seven days. Red Luck Posters were stuck to the door of each home. Meat was marinated and strong rice wine, *ju*, bought. Families arranged visits, and banquets were prepared. In Beijing millions thronged the Temple Fairs to complete their holiday shopping.

The largest *Miaohui* was in Ditan Park. There the noise was deafening. Drums thudded, cymbals clashed and trumpets blared in the cold air. Stall-holders called their wares and customers shouted for children to keep up.

Swept along by the crowds, Mei walked beside her sister, whose mood had darkened. "Why must we come here every year?" Lu moaned. "All these people pushing each other – and where's Mama?"

"She said she wanted to buy something." Mei stood on tiptoe to search but couldn't see her. Red lanterns swayed under the white stone arch of the Sacrifice altar where in times past the emperor would offer sacrifices to earth at the summer solstice, and behind it, more crowds and stalls.

"Fireworks! Fireworks for Spring Festival!"

"Luck Posters to welcome the spring and banish ghosts!"

Dancers on stilts appeared at the end of the lane, accompanied by trumpets and drums. The women wore red satin and waved vast pink fans. The men were in long blue robes and domed hats, beneath which their faces were heavily made up with thickly lined eyes and rouge cheeks. Two children ran in front of them, causing some to wobble. At that moment Mei saw her mother pushing through the crowd with two bottle gourds.

"*Hulu?*" Lu frowned, and uncrossed her arms to take a gourd.

"For luck — and a grandson soon," said Ling Bai.

"Mama!" Lu protested. Her blush of embarrassment was endearing.

"As for you," Ling Bai turned to Mei, "it will protect you against demons."

"I don't need it."

Ling Bai glared at her elder daughter. "Thirty-one years old and no husband? You need a lucky charm."

Lu nudged Mei with her elbow. "Just take it," she whispered.

"*Hulu* is very powerful. Look at the curves. It's heaven and earth in union, true harmony. Especially lucky for a woman," Ling Bai averred.

They walked up the stone steps to the Sacrifice altar where a *jiaozi* theatre was in full swing, musicians playing, in exaggerated ways, trumpets, drums, cymbals and an erhu, a stringed instrument. As four men danced, they tossed a sedan chair – the *jiaozi* – with an actress inside it.

"Where are you going, young wife?" roared the men.

"Going back to my mama's house," sang the actress.

"Where is your husband?"

"At home, like a little boy, with his mother."

The audience laughed. But Lu stood rigid and glared at the spectacle. She loathed folk dancing. Mei glanced at her mother, who was smiling, enjoying the play. Her face was lined and strands of her grey hair flew about her face in the wind. Mei shivered – with cold and guilt. But how could she love if she couldn't forgive? Her father ... She had learned the truth, which had separated her from her mother as completely as if a shutter had fallen between them.

She shook her head, as if to clear it. She wished she could confide in someone, to share the burden ...

"Shall we find some *bingtang hulu*?" asked Ling Bai. Candied-hawthorn-on-a-stick was a favourite winter delicacy that everyone munched at the *Miaohui*.

"Not for me," said Lu. "How can you eat something that's been lying about in this dust for hours?"

The Wangs made their way to the North Gate, Ling Bai searching for a *bingtang hulu* stall.

"People are staring at you," Mei muttered to her sister.

"Are they?"

She sounded indifferent and Mei knew why. Her sister was strikingly beautiful, but never gave it a thought. It was of interest only to others.

Ling Bai bought two *bingtang hulu*, one for Mei and one for herself. They ate them as they walked. The path leading to the North Gate was packed with stalls. A man was pouring tea from a large copper pot with a very long spout. Smoke rose from kebab braziers, the scent of cumin and chilli in the air. Colourful windmills spun, and red lanterns dangled, like giant fruit, from leafless branches.

An ice slide stood in the middle of North Gate Square, children and adults squealing and laughing as they glided down. A long queue snaked round the ticket booth. Bright banners displaying *miyu*, riddles, hung from the trees, where a large crowd had gathered.

Ling Bai and Mei liked *miyu*. Some years ago, when Mei was still a girl, they had competed on National Day and won prizes.

"There's one," said Mei, reading aloud, "A good beginning – a foreign currency." She thought for a while. "The answer is US dollars – *mei yuan. Mei* means 'beautiful' and *yuan* can mean 'beginning'," she whispered to Ling Bai.

"Oh, yes!" exclaimed her mother. "Write it down and we'll win a prize."

"One won't get us far. We'll need to solve at least ten to win something worthwhile."

"We have plenty of time." She glanced at Lu.

"I'm tired of standing about in the cold," said Lu gently. It wasn't a complaint. "We've been out for hours."

"Perhaps you're right," Ling Bai said, clutching her shopping-bag.

Lu took her mother's arm. "It's the same every year."

They heard a drumroll from the direction of the Sacrifice altar and someone shouted, "Lion Dance!" The crowd surged.

Mei, Lu and Ling Bai walked out of the North Gate, where taxis were delivering revellers to the fair. Lu found an empty one and got in, her mother following. Mei sat next to the driver.

"Where to?" cried the driver, jovially.

"The Grand Hotel," said Lu.

He started the engine and turned on the meter. "Which way shall I go? Changan Boulevard is at a standstill."

"Whichever way's the quickest," said Lu, with a hint of impatience.

At the Grand Hotel, they sat at a table with a white linen cloth in the Red Wall café. The waitress brought tea in a silver pot, and as she set it down, the china tinkled. She went away, then returned with cappuccino for Lu.

The café had a high ceiling, crystal lights and a spiral staircase with a vine growing up the banister. Potted plants and panoramic windows gave the impression of a lush conservatory. A waiter brought western cakes on a trolley, so perfect they might have been made of plastic.

"Too beautiful to eat." Ling Bai eyed them. Mei ordered a yellow piece with icing sugar. She hoped it was cheesecake, which she had eaten once before and liked.

Lu stirred her coffee. "They were saying there'll be snow tomorrow."

"I'm not surprised. This is the time of Big Chill, the coldest two weeks of the year," said Ling Bai.

Sitting in the café, Mei found that hard to believe. They were insulated here from the outside world.

Lu took out her mobile phone. "Li-ning is having lunch at the China Club. Maybe he could join us if they've finished."

Mei and Ling Bai sipped their tea, awkward together now that Lu's attention was elsewhere. Mei gazed out of a window, her strong nose and firm mouth making her profile sharp. The sky was darker, the clouds dense, and traffic thick as mud idled on Changan Boulevard. She stretched for a glimpse of Tiananmen Square, which was not far way, but couldn't see it.

"Can't you come for a few minutes?" Lu said, into the phone. She sounded annoyed.

"When do you leave for Canada?" Mei asked her mother, although she knew the date. She was embarrassed that Ling Bai was eavesdropping on Lu's conversation.

"In a week, I think," said Ling Bai, gloomily. "Will I see you before I go?"

"You know that Gupin, my assistant, is going home for Spring Festival. I'm afraid I'll be too busy," Mei said to her tea cup rather than her mother.

Ling Bai sighed. "You should think of finding a new assistant. I thought you were doing well – why keep a migrant worker in the office, especially a man? People will talk."

"I don't care what anyone says. Gupin is good at his job. Unlike some, he has a high-school diploma and is taking evening classes at the university." Suddenly she was picturing Gupin's chiselled face and muscular shoulders in her mind's eye. She wondered what he was doing this weekend. Perhaps he was still at work on the case of the boy who had died in hospital during a routine operation. Perhaps he had been shopping for his sick mother – he may even have been at the *Miaohui*, buying Beijing treats to take home. The thought made her smile.

Lu shut her phone. "I'm sorry. Li-ning won't be able to come, even though he wants to. They're going to the driving range with Big Boss Dong."

"He's always busy." Mei had remembered the last dinner Li-ning couldn't make.

"Everyone wants to collaborate with him on their projects or persuade him to invest. It's hard to be a tycoon."

"Surely – "

"I don't mind. I know what it takes to be a success. He has to put a great deal of time and effort into networking, which means making sacrifices in our personal life. I have to do the same for my show," Lu said. She hosted a programme on Beijing TV in which she interviewed and offered counselling to people who had problems like adulterous affairs or difficult mothers-in-law. It had proved popular, and for a time there had been talk about broadcasting it nationally.

"You both work so hard I hardly see you," Ling Bai said, looking first at Lu, then at Mei. "Especially you."

"Mama, you know everyone wants their case solved yesterday."

"Opportunity! It's everywhere, these days. If you don't grab it someone else will." Lu raised a hand to silence Mei, who had been about to interrupt. "I don't know how much you make, Mei, catching cheating husbands, but for us, lost opportunity might cost millions. So we work all the time, trying to keep up. Li-ning and I know we're being unfair to our family and friends," she laid a hand affectionately on her mother's, "and that's why this Spring Festival, we're taking Mama with us to Vancouver to see Li-ning's family."

She turned to Mei. "Mama told me you've stopped going to see her since she came out of the hospital."

"You've done no better." Mei stole an uneasy glance at Ling Bai.

"I'm busy. I have my show, I lecture and sometimes I travel overseas with my husband. And the *yichuo* – you can't imagine! Dinners, lunches, parties, going to the theatre and the opera with business contacts. If we never said no, we'd be working twenty-four hours a day. But Mama's been to us for dinner. We've gone shopping together." Lu glanced at Ling Bai. "We've grown closer since she had her stroke. What happened last spring made me realise that we can't take anything for granted. One day we will lose her and then we'll wish we'd looked after her properly."

Mei couldn't contradict her but neither could she explain. She was silent, swirling the tea in the bottom of her cup.

"Have you heard," said Ling Bai, eager to defuse the tension, "Hu Bin's been released."

"Wasn't he one of the student leaders at Tiananmen?"

Ling Bai nodded. "Mei knew him at university, didn't you?"

"I met him a couple of times on campus," said Mei. She had seen it in small print on page twenty-one of today's *Beijing Daily*. Hu Bin had been sentenced to twelve years for leading the student protest in 1989. His release, three years early, might mean he was ill.

Hu Bin's release had brought back uncomfortable memories. She had already been working at the police headquarters – the Ministry for Public Security – when the students had taken to the streets in the spring of 1989. Every day she had read avidly about the protest in the square, but unlike millions of other office and factory workers in the city, she had not gone out to join them. She had sat behind her desk at the ministry, ensconced on the other side, the side which in the end went against the students. To this day, she reproached herself for that. The guilt for not having being with those she cared about lodged in her heart like a stone. But how could she have known it would end in blood? That people would die, and friends like Hu Bin would be imprisoned for so long?

She could reproach herself for so much. It had been her, really, she reflected, who had stolen her father's life. Their mother had denounced him for criticising Mao's policies during the Cultural Revolution, the only way to save her children from the labour camp. Her evidence had helped send him to prison, where he died young. When Mei stumbled on the truth last year, while uncovering an ancient jade lost since the Cultural Revolution, she had at first been angry, but then she had grieved. Hatred threatened to destroy her love for her mother. Mei wished she could forgive the woman who had made such great sacrifices and given Mei life twice.

Her mother's voice brought her back to the Red Wall café.

"It's a goodwill gesture, I suppose, to release him before the holiday."

"I'm sure that's right," said Lu, finishing her coffee. "It's about time too. Such ancient history. It's better for both sides to forget."

"It's only been nine years," retorted Mei.

"Exactly. Ancient history." Lu tossed her hair over a shoulder and laughed. "My dear sister, you live too much in the past, and everyone else has moved on. How does the old proverb go? 'The present is like gold.'"

At that moment, the waiter brought their cakes. For a while, they gazed, awestruck and silent, at the art on their plates. Then Mei took a bite of hers and shuddered. It was lime, not cheesecake, and she didn't like lime.

"Lu's right," Ling Bai said to Mei, through a mouthful of her Napoleon. "You must forget the past and move on. Don't carry it with you. Learn to forgive."

Mei's heart jumped. Did her mother know that she had found out what had happened to her father?

"Will you go back to Ya-ping?"

Mei sighed. "But you didn't like him – you didn't want me to marry him."

"That was years ago when he was only a student from the provinces. He's a successful businessman now, living in Chicago."

"He's also divorced."

"So is Li-ning." Ling Bai gazed proudly at her younger daughter. "It may make him a better husband."

Mei took another bite of her cake. "Once a cup's broken, it can't be mended."

"That's because you don't want to mend it," said Lu. "He broke your heart, yes, but that's more ancient history. Live in the present. It's the key to happiness."

"And you can let me worry about my love life." What if she couldn't learn to forgive and forget?

Lu gestured to the waiter for the bill, then said to Mei, "But I care about you because you're my sister. A friend of mine will call you tomorrow. His name is Mr Peng. He's the chairman of Guanghua Record Company. He might have a case for you – a big one."

"Thank you," said Mei. Her sister had irritated her with the unsolicited advice, but she had just redeemed herself.

2

Eight months earlier

"You must thank the Communist Party," said Deputy Yao.

No one called him Grasshopper now. His skinniness had given way to middle-aged padding. He no longer beat the prisoners. Instead he spoke of humane treatment and modernisation. Like the rest of the country, *lao gai* camps were undergoing reform. Deputy Chen didn't believe the rhetoric. Sometimes, he let a beating pass without reprimand – the young guards were keen to do their best, he told his boss at the ministry. But he was ambitious so he followed the Party's orders.

He sat behind his desk, straight as a pencil. His eyes had not changed. They were as chilling as ever.

Lin crouched on a small wooden stool, head bowed.

"You've wasted many good years because you stood against the People."

"I know." Lin was clutching a small bundle as if it were a baby. His eyes were blank. His face was rough and reddened by the desert wind.

"The Party is giving you a second chance to serve the People," said Deputy Yao. "But remember, reform never ends. You must continue after your release. Anti-revolutionary sentiment runs deep in you, even though you have served your full sentence. You must struggle against it always."

"*Shi*," answered Lin.

"You may go now."

"Thank you."

"Don't thank me, thank the Party."

Lin got up. They had given him a Mao jacket and a pair of peasant trousers. The clothes fitted badly. A guard of the age Lin had been when he was arrested led him through the barracks. The prisoners had gone to work at the lime kiln, their cells empty, blankets neatly folded.

Lin stumbled like an old man, trying to keep up. The silence was frightening. Since he had been told of his release, he had had the feeling that something terrible was about to happen and that he would not leave the camp after all. When he had excavated lumps of lime from the bottom of the kiln, he had feared that it would collapse, as had happened to Little Soldier. He feared lime spattering into his eyes, not the blindness that would result but the pain. He couldn't get the image out of his mind of Hu Wei rolling on the ground, screaming, trying to gouge out his own eyes when it had happened to him.

The guard opened the door and Lin walked into the yard alone.

Hot air scorched his face. He felt dizzy. The ground seemed to move beneath his feet. High walls and wire fencing encircled him. Lin tried to steady himself. He felt as if he was in a different place, a place he did not know, even though everything about it was familiar. He took a step forward, two steps, three.

The guard opened the gate. Lin lowered his head. At any moment, someone would come up from behind and haul him back in, he knew. He counted his steps ... one hundred and sixty-eight, one hundred and sixty-nine, one hundred and seventy ... past the gate ... two hundred and one ... three hundred and two. He was in open country.

Four hundred. He stopped and turned around. The gate had closed. He stared at the high walls and barbed wire baking under the sun. The brilliance burned his eyes.

"Hey!" someone shouted.

He spun round and saw a donkey cart.

"Hey!" the driver called again. "Or are you going to walk?"

Lin clutched his bundle and squinted. Why was the man there? And why was he talking to him? He looked around. There was nothing but the sun and the arid landscape.

Then he understood. The donkey cart had come to take him away. He climbed in. The driver spat, hit the donkey with his whip, and shouted, "*Jia*." They were off.

"How many years?" the driver asked. He was a young peasant with brown skin and burly arms. The brim of his straw hat was worn.

"Eight." Lin took off his Mao jacket and folded it carefully. His body, beneath an old vest he had mended many times, was hard and strong after years of labour.

"A long time," the driver observed. "What did you do?"

Lin didn't answer. He fixed his eyes on the land that stretched in front of him, barren, mountainous.

"Things have changed," said the driver after a while. "You go five hundred *li* and see foreigners in Jiayuguan. The townspeople tell me that big Japanese buses come. They're tall as houses and have cold air inside them."

"Hmm." Lin had no idea what the driver was talking about.

"One day, I'll go and see. We had a long-distance bus, but it broke down. No one knows when it can be fixed. I'll take you to the railway station, yes?" He paused. "Will your family come to take you home?"

"I don't think so."

"How will you get there?"

"I'll find a way."

"Where is your home?"

"Beijing."

The driver looked at Lin and his bundle. "You won't get there."

They rode on. The donkey snorted. The wheels squeaked. Lin didn't bother to ask why he had said that. He had long since stopped caring what others said.

"Do you know my brother?" asked the driver.

Lin shook his head.

"He's your cook. He helped me get this donkey cart. It's the only one in the county. We know people want to leave. There's nothing around here for them. The quarry's no good, never has been. All the time people die, lose a leg or an eye. It's hard work for almost no money. You can't build a house or buy a bride.

"The People's Commune's no better. The Communist Party says, 'The People's will is higher than heaven.' Well, an arm can't wrestle a leg. You can't grow anything in sand. The lime kiln was good – until they built the *lao gai* camp and made the prisoners work at it for nothing. But the *lao gai* camp turned out to be good for us. The camp pays me to move people with my donkey cart. Maybe soon I'll have enough for a bride."

Li listened, but heard only a word here, a sentence there. His ears, eyes and throat were numb.

"You don't say much, do you?" The driver was staring at him.

Lin lifted the end of his vest to wipe the sweat off his face.

"How old?" asked the driver, handing him an old water-bottle.

"Twenty-eight."

"You have a woman?"

"No."

Lin swallowed water. It smelled of metal and was too warm. He looked back. In the distance, the *lao gai* camp was like a child's sandcastle. Lin screwed the top tightly on to the water-bottle. In front of him he could see more mountains in the distance, and dreamed of shade.

᠈ᡜ

The railway station was lonely, one hut and a single track. The heat seemed to have sucked the life out of everything around it. The grass beside the track was dry, and iron ore rusted on the hot gravel.

The station master, a man in his forties with a skewed mouth and a black moustache, sat at a table with a deck of cards. Like Lin, he was wearing a white vest. It had two holes, each the size of a coin. He put down the cards and looked at Lin. His eyes went first to Lin's shaven head, then to his face, up and down his body, to his new shoes and his bundle. "What are you doing here?"

"I want to catch a train."

"No passenger trains from here, only freight."

"The donkey-cart man brought me. He said the long-distance bus has broken down."

"That idiot. He's never done an honest day's work in his life — he won't go into the quarry because it's too hard. Everyone else does, though. I ruined my leg there. A rock cut my thigh." He shook his head. "Some people think only of money, like him and his brother. Bringing you here for a train? He swindled you."

Lin dropped his bundle and squatted, burying his head in his hands. The air was like glue. "What am I to do? How can I get away from here?"

As Lin had walked out of East Wind Lao Gai Camp, he had been frightened. The sight of the camp, the shriek of crows, the shadow of clouds, had all startled him. He feared the guards would come after him and drag him back. His nerves, like his freedom – so hard-earned – were fragile.

"You wait for the bus to be mended, or you walk to Yumen, a hundred and twenty kilometres from here." The station master paused, then asked, "What were you in for? Not rape? I hate rapists." He worked a finger inside his nose, drilling deep, eyes squinted, forehead wrinkled.

What a simple soul, Lin thought. Had Lin been a rapist, he would not have been talking to the station master. He would have been executed.

All Lin wanted was to be as far away from this forsaken place as possible. He thought of bribing the man. But what with? He had no possessions. Eventually he stood up, pulled out a roll of paper. He removed his release certificate, then picked out a ten-yuan note. He had no idea how much or little it would buy. He had been given only fifty yuan.

"Please help me," he said, holding out the money.

"What's that for? The camp hasn't taught you much. You think I'm like that crook with the donkey-cart or those men you were with in the camp? Criminal once, criminal all your life. Get out!" The station master stood up and pointed at the open door.

Lin took his bundle and went. He put the money back into his trousers and squatted on the shady side of the hut. The heat engulfed him. Everywhere he looked, he saw white sunshine and no refuge. His head hurt.

He had regular headaches. Sometimes the camp doctor said it was the "hot wind", sometimes the "cold wind". Lin suspected he didn't know what it was. When the pain came, it split his head like a knife, dizzying him. The doctor gave him aspirin, but it didn't help. Headaches didn't count as illness in the *lao gai* camp: the guards beat him when he collapsed at the lime kiln, breaking his nose, teeth and once his elbow, then locked him in the "black cell" for dodging work.

In the distance, he heard a faint whistle. He looked up. A column of white steam rose from behind a mountain ridge.

The station master came out of his hut. He glanced at the incoming train, then at Lin. "I don't want your money and I don't want you to do anything illegal."

"I'm sorry. I didn't mean to offend you. I've been in the camp for eight years and just want to go home."

"The train comes for the quarry and the lime kiln. It stops and loads. Don't jump into one of the wagons like the peasants do. It's against the law – and it isn't right to travel without paying. But talk to the driver, explain about the bus. He may take you with him in the cab."

Lin jumped up, his heart beating fast. "Thank you."

"You aren't on the train yet," the station master reminded him.

3

For once the weather forecast had been accurate. Snow, the fifth fall of the winter, arrived before dawn, and by morning it had thrown a thick blanket over the city. Bicycles parked on pavements disappeared. Snowploughs, their drivers exhausted before the morning rush-hour, stopped at verges. The few buses that ran were packed. Trucks and cars skidded out of control. Some were stranded, others broke down.

It seemed a miracle to Mei that her little red Mitsubishi got through. She arrived at her office shortly after ten and made a pot of Oolong tea. Then she looked at the pile of paper on Gupin's desk and felt anxious again about his holiday. Much work had still to be done on the boy who had died in hospital. There were interview notes and medical records to examine, facts to check and connections to make.

She wanted to page Gupin, but she knew there was no point: he might be stuck on a bus. She brought the papers to her desk. Gupin had drawn arrows and question marks on one of the computer printouts. She wondered what they meant.

The phone rang and she snatched up the receiver. It wasn't Gupin.

"My name is Peng Datong," an unfamiliar voice said. "I'm a friend of your sister Lu. You and I met once, at her wedding. I'm the president of Guanghua Record Company. I need your help. Lu said you're one of the best private investigators in Beijing. Can you come to my office?"

"Now?"

"Yes. It's urgent. I'll send my driver to pick you up."

"What's the problem?"

"Not on the phone. My secretary will meet you at the door to our building and bring you to my office. Please hurry."

Mei hung up, then paced her office, trying to think. Mr Peng's tone had unsettled her. She knew she couldn't say no to a man like him – he had made that clear – but she resented it.

"Where is Gupin?" She looked at her wristwatch. Nearly eleven. Now she paged Gupin and left her mobile-phone number with the girl at the service centre.

Mr Peng's secretary did not introduce herself. She didn't even look at Mei. She was a chubby woman in her early twenties, tightly wrapped in a pink suit. She led Mei through brightly lit corridors on a pair of pink high heels. Doors opened and shut. People rushed past them, greeting each other or shouting, carrying posters and videotapes or pushing trolleys loaded with magazines. Some said hello. Still Miss Pink said nothing.

A pair of pearl earrings dangled from her lobes, like fish flipping out of water, catching Mei's eye. Mei could see her neck, porcelain white. She wondered how it would feel to touch it.

The lift took them up twenty-two floors to the top. The doors opened and they stepped into an office. Two lamps with silk shades glowed on a desk, behind which stood filing cabinets and a leather chair. Mei guessed that this was where Miss Pink sat.

Miss Pink led her through a large leather-covered door into an enormous room with floor-to-ceiling windows and a large mahogany desk.

"Red tea. Make it strong," said a tired voice. A tall leather chair turned slowly. A man with an angular face, a shock of bushy hair, a white shirt and dark suit was sitting in it.

"Yes, sir," Mei heard Miss Pink say. That she could speak, and so sweetly, almost surprised her.

Mr Peng's eyes were red and unfocused. "Thank you for coming."

Mei took a seat in front of the desk. The leather upholstery felt springy and new.

For a while they sat in silence – waiting, it seemed to Mei, for Mr Peng to wake up.

Miss Pink returned with a tea tray. She put it on Mr Peng's desk and poured two cups. Mr Peng took his. "That's all," he told his secretary. His long thin lips veered downward when he spoke.

A glance passed between them. Mei saw Miss Pink's eyes grow warm. She handed the second cup to Mei and left, heels clicking.

Mr Peng picked up a remote control that lay on his desk and switched on the television. A music video began to play, images of rivers, mountains, bamboo forest in a gale. A sword fight faded to a woman singing, beautiful, longing, tearful.

"She's pretty, isn't she?" said Mr Peng. "Not conventionally so, perhaps, but she could tear you apart with those eyes. And that voice – remarkable!"

Mei didn't say anything.

"You don't know who she is, do you?" Mr Peng sipped some tea.

"No."

"That's Kaili, our newest star. But you must have heard the song. It's the theme to the movie *Knights of Heaven*."

"Sorry." Mei hadn't seen the movie. In fact, she hadn't seen a movie for a long time.

Bamboo forests and a river view gave way to a wedding, then a journey, snow, and Kaili with a voice like a fire. Mr Peng switched off the video.

"At the moment Kaili is our most important star. One day she could be as big as Tian Tian." Mr Peng paused. "But she's disappeared."

"What do you mean?"

"We can't find her. She's missed appointments. She hasn't been to her apartment. No one's seen or heard from her. We're being bombarded with phone calls from journalists asking what's happened to her. And she's booked to perform at the Spring Festival gala in two weeks! We must find her."

"How long has it been?"

"Four days."

"Why did you wait until now to contact me?"

"At first we thought it was another of her episodes. When she didn't turn up, her assistant checked the spas and nightclubs she uses, spoke to people she knows, and I've been to her apartment."

"When you say 'another of her episodes', what do you mean?"

"It's happened before – a few times. She's gone off without a word, sometimes for a day or two, sometimes longer."

"What happened on those occasions?"

"Either we found her or she just reappeared. You know what these pop stars are like, with their whims and moods. Kaili's a great singer, with plenty of charisma – and the artistic temperament – but a year ago we found her in Xiehe Hospital. She'd taken an overdose."

"Is she an addict?"

"She uses drugs, sometimes worse than others. Often it's not her fault. There are too many bad influences in her circle."

Mr Peng took out a packet of cigarettes and a gold lighter. "Last Wednesday she did a show at the Capital Gymnasium. Manyu, her assistant, will fill you in on the details. Kaili disappeared afterwards."

"What about her family? Maybe they know where she is."

"Her parents live in Hangzhou and she has nothing to do with them." Mr Peng tossed a folded piece of paper across his desk. "Still, I sent them a telegram in case they knew anything. They didn't – here's their reply."

Mei picked it up. It had been dispatched yesterday afternoon at four fifteen, addressed to Mr Datong Peng, CEO, Guanghua Record Company, 356 Fuchang Boulevard, Beijing. It read:

DO NOT KNOW WHERE KAILI IS STOP WHAT IS WRONG
QUESTION MARK GANG KANG

Mr Peng lit a cigarette. "I wasn't surprised. They haven't spoken to each other for years. Her parents disowned her when she dropped out of university. When I met her, she was living in Beijing with a businessman."

"Have you been in touch with the police?"

"Of course not. I can't let it be known that I've lost one of my biggest stars!"

The telephone rang. Mr Peng frowned. He waited for it to stop. When it didn't, he grabbed the receiver. "I said no calls!" he exploded. "Tell her I'm busy … say I'm in a meeting – damn it, I *am* in a meeting." He looked as if he wanted to slam it down – his hands shook with the urge to do so. But something held him back. He picked up a pen and tapped it on his desk. "All right, put her through."

"Hello, baby, what's wrong?" he said calmly, a smile floating up to his face. "How come you're not at school?"

Mei felt awkward to be listening to a private conversation. But Mr Peng seemed to have forgotten she was there. He had relaxed in his chair and was twisting a gold pen, watching the light bounce off it.

"Your ma's crying. Why? Let me talk to her."

Mei looked out of the window. It was still snowing.

She heard Mr Peng say, "Don't worry, baby. Your ma has a tiny hole in her heart. She can't breath if she's upset … I've been working, baby. We're always busy at this time of year. Your ma knows that. You understand why I'm doing this, don't you? It's for you and Ma.

"I'm going to give you a very special present at Spring Festival … No, better than that … You'll have to wait. Now, you go to school, and I'll try to come home tonight … I can't promise, but I'll try. Talk to Mama. Maybe the two of you can go to Hong Kong and do some holiday shopping next week."

Mr Peng hung up and tossed the pen on to his desk. "My daughter. She's a clever girl, fourteen this year. It's a shame she doesn't do well at school. Her mother neglects her. That woman! I've given her everything she could possibly want – a big apartment, a house in the country, a car, a driver, three maids – but she claims she's ill all the time. Headaches, shortness of breath, her heart … She's had all sorts of treatments – Chinese medicine, acupuncture, cupping. One of the maids spends most of the day boiling herbs for her. Do you remember last year's fad for fungus drinks? You grow it in some potion and eventually drink the juice. My wife had so many jars of it that they took over the apartment. It looked like a laboratory filled with jellyfish in tanks.

"She's mad, and a bad influence on my daughter. But what can I do? I'm at work all the time. Do you think I should send my daughter to a boarding-school? Some people tell me I should."

Mr Peng got up and walked to the windows. He was short but perfectly proportioned. His face was well shaped and flat. His eyes were small but they didn't droop. The combination of these elements, though, was dull, as if whoever had assembled him had selected them at random. Nothing looked right. His bushy hair, which might have looked youthful on another man, suggested only debauchery on his.

Mr Peng watched the snow as if he'd never seen it before.

Eventually he said grimly, "Miss Wang, I need you to find Kaili. I'm worried. This isn't like her and there have been no reported sightings. For someone like her, that's almost impossible."

"Do many people know of her disappearance?"

"In the company, only Manyu and I. Others might have guessed that something's wrong."

"What about her friends?"

"She doesn't have any. There are a few hangers-on who sponge off her, but she hates them."

Mr Peng came back to his desk. He opened a drawer. "Here is a key to Kaili's apartment. I want you to see Kaili's assistant. She'll help you to get started."

Mei took it.

He telephoned his secretary "Miss Wang is leaving. Please take her to Manyu."

He stared at Mei. "Find her – please. Telephone me as soon as you have news."

The door opened and Miss Pink was back.

4

Mr Zhang, the freight-train driver, had been running up and down the branch line for twenty-two years. "They call me Old Iron Road — *Lao Tielu*. I've seen everything. The big snow storm of 1982? We were stranded out west for five days. I thought we'd die." Mr Zhang wore a towel round his neck and smoked a pipe filled with tobacco. He wore a railway cap even when he took off his shirt and his chest was bare. It was hot in the cab. He puffed at his pipe, watched Lin feed the furnace, and talked.

"They built the railway into Gansu in the 1950s and 1960s. It was called Discovering and Developing the West. My father was one of those who answered the Party's call. He was from Hangzhou, an engineer. Such a mighty project ... They called it the New Silk Road."

Mr Zhang checked the water level and the thermometer. He leaned out of the cab to see where they were. "Stop shovelling the coal," he said to Lin. "It's time to slow down.

"Three years ago, my father went back to his old village for a visit. He said everything had changed. Every home had a refrigerator and a colour TV. I couldn't believe it. The really rich ones had cars. It's hard to get rich here in Gansu where we only have stones and sand. Is it easy to get rich in Beijing? I suppose everyone already is rich, all those big officials. I've never been to Beijing, but my father went once, for a railway conference. He raved about it for years. He said Beijing's so big you can walk whichever way you like and you won't get out of it. The boulevards were wide enough for five buses together. Maybe I'll go one day, just to see it with my own eyes."

Twilight fell as mist rose from the fields, slowly at first, and then it was dark. They pulled into a freight yard. Lin leaned against the back of the cab, watching the fire die down in the furnace. His face was covered with sweat, his arms and vest smudged black. He rubbed his palms together, looking for the colour of his skin.

"I spend the night here and set off again in the morning," said Mr Zhang. "I can't take you any further. From here to Lanzhou, the railway police are on the lookout. Yumen's about eighty kilometres, not far. Go there and catch a passenger train to Lanzhou."

They said goodbye between an engine and a string of coal trucks.

Lin didn't know whether he should start walking to Yumen straight way or wait until morning. He wandered through the freight yard aimlessly. He didn't even know the way to Yumen.

Two bouncing flashlights approached, a man and a woman in railway uniforms holding them.

"What are you doing here?" The woman shone her light on Lin's face.

"You're not allowed inside the freight yards," added the man.

Lin turned his face sideways.

"This isn't a passenger station." The woman had a round face and straight short hair.

Now the man pointed his light at Lin. "He doesn't want to pay like everyone else has to – damn peasant."

He snatched Lin's bundle. "Give me that!" He rifled through it. "Older Sister, he isn't poor. Look at this." He held up the new Mao jacket the *lao gai* camp had given Lin.

"Get out of here," the woman urged. "If you don't, the freight-yard police will catch you."

"He's a criminal – look at his shaved head – escaped from prison. Worse, maybe he's a saboteur. We should hand him over to the authorities."

"It isn't our job." The woman tugged at his sleeve. "Let's finish putting up the lights and go home. Leave him to the police."

The man threw the bundle at Lin's feet and barked, "Get out of the yard."

The woman twitched his sleeve again and they went, waving their flashlights to let other workers know where they were.

Lin picked up his bundle and moved in the opposite direction, past monstrous black trucks with white characters, like the evil eye, on their sides. He stumbled on the gravel and the uneven track. Sharp stones cut into the straw soles of his shoes. He crossed a track and ran past a row of container wagons. He heard workers shouting some distance away. The glow of a flashlight appeared straight ahead, and he looked for a gap between the wagons, then crossed to the other side.

He mustn't let the freight-yard police catch him. If they did they'd lock him up again. A reformed prisoner was still a criminal.

He wanted to get out of the yard, there were flashlights, everywhere now, and voices.

Lin yanked at the door of a wagon but it was locked. The lights and voices were nearer. He tried another. It moved a little. He threw his entire weight behind it and it slid open. He tossed his bundle inside and climbed up after it.

He shut the door and felt his way to a corner. When his eyes had adjusted to the darkness, he saw dim light under the door, which grew brighter and sharper as he watched. Lin tensed.

Gradually the line dimmed, until he was plunged into total darkness. He shivered. He took out all the clothes he had in his bundle and put them on, wrapping the Mao jacket tightly round himself. He decided to stay where he was till morning, then make his way to Yumen.

Lin curled up in the corner, listening. He heard the cry of an owl, the crackle of tracks as trains raced along them, muffled sounds that might have been men's footsteps or wild animals.

The wagon was empty, but the smell of iron ore lingered. It reminded him of a railway station long ago when he had been young and new to the ocean, when he had travelled home from university, when he had said goodbye to her, when he had lain in front of the train on the fateful night that summer had come too early ...

When Lin woke, it was still dark but the train was moving, the wheels clunking a slow rhythm. He tried to get up, but his feet were numb. He moved to the door, searching with his hands, found the lever and pushed. The door slid open to reveal a moonlit landscape – he distinguished fences, white stone rail markers and, in the distance, an occasional hut, beyond which the jagged mountains rose into the sky.

An icy wind hit him like a shot to the heart, and he fell to his knees.

He was free. He was going home to the city of his childhood memories, to the narrow alleyways and the scent of fried breadsticks on summer mornings, to the crumbling gate and the ancient maple tree – he had hidden little treasures in its cracks.

He held on to the door, teeth chattering. The train was rounding a bend, the engine puffing white clouds. Lin gazed into the distance as the horizon paled. A new morning.

5

Kaili's assistant, Manyu, had an office on the fourth floor of the Guanghua Record Company building. It was a small room with a window that gave on to the street. The walls were bare and a Chinese screen stood in a corner.

When Miss Pink and Mei arrived Manyu was on the phone. She smiled into the mouthpiece and waved them in. "She should be better in a couple of days ... Why should I lie to you? ... Of course, I promise." She hung up and her smile faded. "Press," she said.

Miss Pink introduced Mei: "This is Miss Wang."

Manyu stood up. She was plain, in her late twenties or early thirties. A small nose protruded from her face the same way her breasts protruded from her body. She wore a loose sweater over a checked shirt and grey trousers. Her smile was warm but it didn't produce the effects, as in most women, of making her more attractive. "I've been expecting you." She gestured to the two chairs in front of her desk.

"I'm going back up now," said Miss Pink. She might have included Manyu in this remark but she didn't look at her. "Anything you need, Miss Wang, please call me." She nodded at Mei, turned and left, pink heels clicking.

"Thank you!" shouted Manyu. But Miss Pink had disappeared.

"I don't know how much Mr Peng told you," said Manyu, sitting down.

"Not much."

Manyu nodded, not meeting Mei's eyes. "In that case I'd better start from the beginning. Last week, the China Workers' Association arranged a Celebrate Over-production and Welcome the Spring Festival gala. A lot of famous names were there – Tian Tian, Chen Jung, who had just won an international folk-singing award in Budapest, Big Idiot, Little Idiot and the People's Liberation Army Dance Group. Kaili was the newcomer of the year, one of the stars. She is very popular just now because she sings the theme to *Knights of Heaven*.

"After the show, I went to her dressing room. I took her some honey tea and cigarettes. I didn't stay to chat – she's drained after a performance and prefers not to talk. It can be tricky, but I have to be prepared for whatever mood she's in.

"I left her to check on the stage door. Kaili likes to know how many people are waiting outside to see her – she enjoys that kind of thing. Then I went to alert the driver. I was probably away from her for half an hour."

"That seems a long time."

"Well, I ran into people I knew. In the music industry everyone knows everyone else, especially the assistants and PRs," Manyu stammered.

The telephone rang. Manyu waited for it to stop, but then asked Mei if they could go somewhere else. "I'm afraid there will be more calls – everyone's asking about Kaili. We could go down to the café, if you like."

Mei agreed. Manyu stood up and disappeared behind the screen. She emerged with two large diaries. "I keep Kaili's schedule and run errands for her. These are the records."

The café was in a glass-roofed courtyard, with a rock fountain in the middle, palm trees and ivy. Glass-topped tables with black rims were dotted about the peach-coloured floor.

"The trees are plastic," Manyu explained.

A photographer, a makeup artist and models were wandering around the synthetic greenery. It looked as if a fashion photo shoot was in progress.

A tall waiter in a white shirt and black trousers came over. "What can I get you?" he asked, bowing slightly.

Mei ordered white coffee and Manyu coconut juice. They picked up where they had left off.

"What happened after you got back?" asked Mei.

"I waited outside her dressing room." Manyu stacked the diaries on the table, lining them up exactly.

"Is that usual you didn't go in to check on her?"

"No. I'm not her bodyguard. Sometimes I go in, sometimes I wait for her to call me. How could I have known that she'd disappear? Nothing about her or our surroundings could have alerted me. I did my job as I've done it for two years. I'm a good assistant, conscientious, hard-working and organised. Kaili would tell you so if you could ask her."

"But this isn't about you."

"It feels as if it is. You suspect me of something. Mr Peng thinks I haven't done my job properly. But the past few months have been crazy. Kaili had a lot of gigs, engagements and interviews with the press. I had a lot to deal with, and I'm not good with chaos."

There was a shout from the photo shoot, then a commotion.

"Have you been backstage at a gig, Miss Wang?" Manyu looked at her pleadingly. "It's mad – props, people, costumes, so noisy and crowded. I have to get everything ready, Kaili's outfits, Q-tips, lemon drops, cigarettes, pills. She has to have her tea at just the right temperature, warm, not hot."

"Is Kaili difficult to work with?"

"No. I like my job and the pay's good. I've learned so much about the business, met so many interesting people. It's a great opportunity for me. Kaili isn't easy-going, but celebrities never are. They like things a certain way."

The waiter brought their order, then left them alone again.

"When did you realise that Kaili had gone?" Mei asked.

"When the crowd had cleared, I suppose, around midnight. I hadn't seen her and felt worried so I went to knock on her door. There was no answer. I wasn't sure whether I should go in, but eventually I did and she wasn't there.

"First I thought maybe she'd gone to see someone, but most people had left and their dressing rooms were empty. Then I thought maybe she'd just gone without me, but the car was still there. Our driver was asleep behind the wheel."

"You're sure you were outside her dressing room all the time?"

"Yes – so that she could find me if she wanted me."

"So it was impossible for her to have left without your seeing her?"

"Not necessarily, if she wanted to slip out. But the stage-door guards didn't see her leaving either. I had thought that perhaps she had left with someone else, but if she had, the guards would have noticed."

"Can you take me to the Capital Gymnasium? I'd like to see backstage?"

"Today?"

"The sooner the better."

6

Lin got out of the wagon as soon as the train stopped. Outside, it was hot. He began to walk, glancing back every few steps, but no one was chasing him. The train seemed to have stopped for no reason. Nothing was being loaded or unloaded. In the bright sunshine, it resembled a strand of giant black beads.

After about two miles he came to a station. It consisted of a platform and a one-window ticket office. A battered sign read "Dry Valley". Two brown-skinned young farmhands squatted by some sacks, smoking hand-rolled tobacco. A woman of uncertain age sat on a stool, a basket of boiled eggs at her feet, a towel wrapped round her head. Beside her, a small boy, with a large face and slanting eyes, wore only a pair of oversize cotton trousers with torn knees. From time to time, he giggled. Sometimes he made noises that sounded like words but were unintelligible.

Lin bought a ticket for the next passenger train, a slow one that went east. The man behind the window snorted at his *lao gai* release certificate — the identification paper one had to present to purchase train tickets — but he was either too tired or too hot to delay him. Perhaps he didn't care.

Lin bought an egg, wiped it clean on his vest, tossed the shell to the side of the platform and ate it. Then he realised how hungry he was and bought another. From behind her back, the woman produced an aluminium army water-bottle. She smiled, showing rotten teeth, and offered it to Lin.

"Which province is this?" he asked.

"Gansu," the woman answered.

Still in the highlands, cursed Lin. The land was like a giant hand that, at any moment, might snap closed, trapping him.

He sat down on his bundle near the farmhands, who went on smoking and passing tobacco to each other without a word. The little boy had crawled into the egg woman's lap and was sucking at her breast. Lin stared at the composition of mother and half-naked child. They seemed not to exist as separate bodies but as part of the land and the air.

Cicadas chirped from dry bushes. A vulture that had been gliding above disappeared, probably having found prey. With every breath he took, Lin felt the heat drying him.

Eventually the train came in and he boarded it. The carriages were nearly empty and had wooden benches as seats. From the window, he saw the sunset — a burned disc sinking into grey earth. When night came he lay down, making a pillow of his bundle, but sleep was shallow and short-lived. The seat's narrow bars hurt his bones.

His dreams, when they came, were fragmented and terrifying. There was the blackness of the isolation cell and the foul smell of waste. When the train stopped, the station lights woke him. Again he was scared, and confused. He saw Little Soldier's twisted, bloody face, the horror of his friend's death on the day the lime kiln had collapsed.

Lin felt hot, then cold. He shivered in darkness and daylight.

By the end of the second day, the landscape had changed. The earth was yellow now with jagged plateaux and sandy cliffs. The train was passing through Yellow River country. For a fleeting moment, he felt love for his country. Poems about the great river rushed to his mind, though he could only remember fragments. Youth, he thought nostalgically. What a beautiful word. But what use were words when he had neither hope nor love?

The next morning Lin woke up hungry, with sunbeams pouring through the window. The train was once again in mountains, but this time there were sloping green hillsides, and below them an open landscape of maize and wheat. Mud houses with interlacing dark roofs stood at the edge of the fields.

When the sun rose, a town appeared and the train slowed. A road ran parallel to the tracks. Peasants carried heavy loads on *bian dian* – bamboo poles across their shoulders – wobbling along, passed by donkey carts. Naked children played outside their homes. When they saw the train, they stopped and shouted, "*Houche! Houche!* Fire wagons." Two or three ran alongside the train, their bottoms flashing white in the sunshine.

The train passed more houses where women were hanging out their washing, then stopped at a station. Lin got off. He had travelled as far as his ticket allowed, to the end of the line. He touched the waist of his trousers and felt the crisp banknote, his last ten yuan. He swung his bundle over his shoulder and took a deep breath of warm air.

7

Capital Gymnasium loomed behind the twirling snow. Mei squinted. She could just make out the red flags on its roof. For as long as she could remember, the Capital Gymnasium had been where everything happened, the Ping Pong World Championships, the Communist Party birthday celebrations, the May Day and National Day celebrations and, of course, the Spring Festival evening gala.

It was traditional for families to gather on the eve of the Chinese New Year to feast and watch the Spring Festival evening gala on television. In the countryside, where few families owned a set, villagers and their relatives travelled miles to watch the concert at which the country's most famous actors and singers performed. Top Party officials were always in attendance, and so were special guest stars from Hong Kong or Japan.

A few years ago when Mei was working at the Ministry for Public Security, she had attended the gala. A matchmaker had introduced her to Yuan Yuan, the youngest son of an old revolutionary family, the Chous, who attended the gala every year. They invited Mei to come with them and seated her between the parents. General Chou hardly said a word to her or to anyone else. He sat in his chair with the intensity he might have exerted in conducting a field battle. Yuan Yuan sat on the other side of his mother, bored. Sometimes he clapped to pretend he was enjoying the show like everyone else. Mrs Chou, however, didn't stop talking. She wanted to know everything about Mei: her career, her friends, her values, her opinions on Party politics, her mother, her sister, and what kind of wife she would make.

Afterwards Mei complained about the interrogation to her sister, but Lu said only, "Of course they'd ask you all those questions. They need to be sure that you would be suitable for Yuan Yuan and for their family. Look on it as your good fortune."

Mei wondered what had happened to Yuan Yuan. He had stopped calling her after she'd refused to be the minister's mistress and resigned.

Mei and Manyu walked briskly across the square in front of the Capital Gymnasium. Ahead, a shadow moved in the blizzard. As they came closer they saw it was a young man with a spear. He wore only a tracksuit and no hat. He was waving the spear, and the red tassel at the top fluttered to and fro. Manyu threw Mei a glance. Her eyes seemed to ask, "Why?" Mei wondered too. Who would practise *kung fu* in a snow storm? Maybe the weather was driving people crazy.

They moved on and continued to talk. Mei remembered the key Mr Peng had given her to Kaili's apartment and asked about his relationship with the singer.

Manyu peeped out from under her hood. She looked like a little bird. "Close in what way?"

"You know what I mean. Were they intimate with each other?"

"I don't know. But Mr Peng is involved with Kaili's career, which is good for her. He's very powerful, a star-maker. After all, it was he who discovered Tian Tian."

Mei thought a PA would know whether or not her boss was having an affair. Manyu was not telling the truth. "Are you afraid of Mr Peng?" she asked, suddenly.

Snow fell between them. Manyu looked away. "I do my job and that's all."

They went round to the back of the stadium, which was covered with scaffolding. Piles of bricks, timber and long blue-plastic-wrapped shapes lay inside an area encircled by green plastic netting. A security guard in an orange safety vest squatted on a heap of steel poles, shivering. Workers in padded winter coats and hard hats struggled in the snow, pushing wheelbarrows.

They waited by the stage door for the site manager to let them in.

"Tell me more about Kaili. Does she drink?" Mei pulled her woollen hat over her ears.

"Sometimes at parties. Sometimes on her own."

"A lot?"

"It depends. Well, some parties get out of hand. You can't really … Sometimes … She has her moods."

"What about drugs?"

"No." Manyu was quick and firm. "Kaili doesn't do drugs."

Remembering what Mr Peng had told her about Kaili's past drug problems, Mei was certain now that Manyu was not being truthful. But why? Was she afraid? Was she guilty of some wrong-doing? What was she hiding?

The stage door opened. A man in a dark jacket and tie, clipboard in hand, ushered them inside. He introduced himself as Mr Huang, the site manager. "I'm told to take you to the dressing rooms – is that right? What do you want to see?"

"I don't know yet," said Mei.

Mei and Manyu peeled off their padded jackets, hats and gloves. Mei stamped the snow off her boots, making loud echoes.

Mr Huang led them into a long corridor where workers were plastering and painting the walls while a foreman, with his hands on his hips, shouted instructions.

"Modernisation," said Mr Huang. "The building is forty years old. Next year the whole place will be refurbished, which means we'll have to close for a while."

A group of five or six young men were squatting along the wall, eating rice and noodles from their lunchboxes. They stopped talking to stare at the visitors. Further along, electricians pulled cables and shouted for tools as they worked on the lights.

"Are you the only ones here today?" Mr Huang barked at one. "Lunch already? You can't leave until the work's done!"

The man stood up. "It's the weather. Many live far away."

"I'll cut your pay if you don't finish in time for the Spring Festival gala."

A minute later, Mei heard the foreman hurrying his men back to work.

"Where do you find your workers?" Mei asked Mr Huang.

"They come from all over the place. The electricians are from Beijing, some from villages outside the city, in Chang Ping or Ping Gu. Others are migrants from the provinces, farmhands. They're cheap and they work hard. But you get what you pay for. Quality is a problem." He spat. "Construction used to be a respectable profession, state employment, with good pay. No longer. These days, everyone's found a better way of making money and no one is willing to sweat and labour. I was once an old Construction Hand. We had proper skills."

The corridor grew narrower and darker. The few windows were covered with dirty sheets, and wooden boards were piled at the foot of the wall. Mei watched the migrant workers chipping, hammering and painting. She thought again of Gupin. He had worked on construction sites when he first came to Beijing. She imagined now that he was one of these men, sweat dripping off his forehead. A chill ran through her: Gupin was never late – and he still hadn't been in touch – maybe something bad had happened to him this morning.

They turned into a bare, dark corridor. A few stage props, empty chairs, two folding tables, a ladder, two mops and a bucket had been left lying around. Mr Huang pulled a string that hung from the ceiling. Neon tubes flickered and shone.

"The dressing rooms." Mr Huang waved a hand at the row of doors.

"This was Kaili's," Manyu pointed to one.

Mei went in and switched on the light. There was no window. The room was empty but for a white shirt hanging from a hook on the wall. Mei took it down. It was a man's, size large, frayed at the collar and hem. The label read "Great Beauty".

"When was the last performance?" she called to Mr Huang.

"Yesterday."

Mei held the shirt to her nose but it smelled of nothing in particular. She put it back on the hook.

"The dressing rooms have just been cleaned," he added.

The ceiling lights gave out a soft glow. A musty smell hung in the air. It was clear that there was only one way to get in and out of the place, through the door. How had Kaili got out without being seen? Mei asked herself, staring at her reflection in the mirror.

A faint hammering distracted her. She left the room and went down the corridor.

"But the stage is that way!" Manyu called.

Mei walked on towards where the noise was coming from. At the end, the corridor had been sealed off with a temporary wall and a sign: "Construction Site. No Entry." She listened but heard nothing on the other side of the partition.

8

The town, Nanguan, had a main street. The houses on it were mud-built but for the Hall of the Town Revolutionary Committee and Town Security, which was brick. There were a few shops – a general store, a grocer, a butcher, a herbalist, a confectioner and tea merchant and two huts selling spring-onion pancakes and *wotou*.

It was market day. Peasants walked briskly, with vegetable baskets hanging from *bian dian*. Women carried bamboo panniers in their arms or on their heads. Ox and donkey carts transported pigs, chickens and people. Every hundred yards another group were huddled over bicycles and donkey carts, trying to fix chains and tyres. An old bus had broken down outside the hall. The driver had the bonnet up and was tinkering with the engine. A group of men surrounded him, some watching, others offering advice.

Lin bought lunch at a food stall, two *wotou* and a large bowl of *pao mo* – shredded steamed buns in broth. The *wotou* were unlike the ones he'd had in the *lao gai* camp. They were warm and made from fresh maize flour. Lin watched the traffic as he ate. Young men in their best shirts and polyester trousers passed in groups. Girls held hands and giggled. Two peasants with long braids went by on a donkey cart. They looked about sixteen, their breasts silhouetted beneath light tops. He felt a melancholy lust stir.

Across the road, a travelling barber sat on a folding chair waiting for customers. Lin went over. "How much?"

"Shave, cut and wash, five yuan."

Lin nodded an "okay". The barber indicated the chair.

"Leave your bundle on the ground," he said, sharpening a cut-throat razor on a piece of leather. "I'll keep an eye on it."

But Lin held on to his belongings.

"Have you travelled far, brother?" the barber asked.

"Yes."

"Where from and where are you going?"

Lin thought about it. "From Gansu."

"You don't speak with a Gansu accent."

"Laojia is not Gansu." Lin amended his story. "My home town is further west, up in the Qinghai highlands."

The barber wet his face with a towel. He had wide-apart eyes that stretched further still further when he smiled. "What brings you here?"

"I need work."

"What kind?"

"It doesn't matter. I just want to make enough money for a train ticket to Beijing."

"Every young man wants to go to the city," said the barber, lathering Lin's beard. "I don't blame them. Rich people live in the cities, the poor in the countryside. You'll never get rich farming, with the quotas, more quotas, the national tax and the county tariff. When you have a good year, they slap on a good-harvest levy, and when the weather's bad, you're done for. You can't feed the old or the young. It isn't easy to make a living when you're relying on the weather. Lean back, brother. If I were as young as you, I'd leave too. Don't move. The razor's coming down. What kind of work did you do at home?"

"I was in a lime kiln."

"No lime kilns here, just farms. Thank heaven I don't work in the fields. I'm a small-skills person. I don't expect to get rich, but as long as I've got my razor, I can feed my family. I have two children," he put up two fingers. "One girl, one boy. When my wife had the second, the county fined us four thousand yuan for violating the one-child policy. I might be a small-skills person but I went in and threw the cash in their faces. I've a son. That's all I care about. The flame of my ancestors will continue to burn!"

When the barber had finished, he took out a pink compact, opened it and held up the mirror in front of Lin, who caressed his chin. It felt smooth and soft. He stared at the strange face in the mirror. He could almost see the young man he used to be.

The barber was washing his razor in a wooden bucket when Lin handed him the money. He looked up, squinting. "Many young men have gone to the cities. Now, at harvest time, there's too much work for the women and the old. If you don't mind hard work, there's plenty in the fields. But you won't be paid much."

The barber's advice rang in Lin's ears as he wandered among the market's customers. He thought about trying for work in one of the shops — after all, he'd been to university. But they might need to see his release paper. Then he wouldn't find any work at all.

The crowd kept the vendors busy. Their goods were laid out on straw mats, like treasure: fashionable leather bags and belts, cosmetics, and hair-clips in many colours and shapes from coastal provinces.

The two girls from the donkey cart were looking at scarves.

"The red one would suit you," said Lin. The scarves reminded him of home. He remembered girls wearing them in Beijing.

The girl turned. She was small and dark-skinned with a pointed chin and wild eyes.

"You're supposed to wear it like this." He turned the scarf over so that the patterns showed their true colours and tied it on for her.

"I know." She jerked away from him.

Her bigger, chubbier friend smiled at Lin. Her expression was as innocent as a child's and seemed to say, "She's always like that."

"Twenty yuan," said the vendor.

"How much?" the pretty girl shrieked, but she didn't take off the scarf.

"It's imported. Look at the label — Korean. You don't find prints like this in China."

"Ten."

"I have to travel to Chengdu to buy them and they're expensive anyway. If you don't want it, others will."

"It's too much," her friend murmured.

But, as if she was under a spell, the girl couldn't leave the scarf.

"It's Little Sister Xue!" Three youths appeared, one in a multi-coloured polo shirt and a pair of aviator sunglasses. His companions were shorter and thinner. The smallest's eyes were bloodshot – he'd been drinking.

"But can you afford it?" The man with sunglasses pulled the girl's scarf. He had muscular arms and a red neck.

"That's none of your business!" She tried to free herself from him, but he held on.

"If you tear it, you pay!" bellowed the vendor.

"Perhaps I should buy it for you." He pulled her towards him and shoved his face into hers.

The chubby girl screamed, "Stop it!" She was trying to come to her friend's rescue but the other men held her fast. Red Eye gave a strange snort.

The petite girl struggled, twisting violently. Her right arm was pinned behind her back, but with her free hand she swung at her attacker, hitting his shoulder and face. His sunglasses fell off. He was laughing. He pushed his face to hers, and she spat into his eyes.

"Whore! Other men get into your trousers, I can't get a kiss!" He wiped his face with the back of his hand, then clenched a fist and swung it at her. Her eyes widened and she flinched. She was like a horse that knew a blow was coming because it was used to beatings. Briefly her face showed a sadness that made her look ten years older and heartbreakingly beautiful.

Lin approached like a gust of wind, his fist as hard as a stone. With one blow, he had knocked the man down. He fell on to a display of hairpins and cosmetics boxes, crushing them beneath his weight. The vendor screamed and so did the girls. The other two men hurled themselves at Lin. Red Eye jumped up and grasped him while the other man struck his face. Lin's teeth snapped shut and he heard a crack.

Lin shook off Red Eye, then threw him to the ground. He punched the other man, who shrieked and fell to his knees, then kicked him. Red Eye got up and hit Lin from behind, but Lin hardly feel the blows. All he could see was the coward at his feet. Suddenly he felt an overwhelming urge to kill the man. The thought of squeezing the life out of him with his own hands filled him with excitement. He pounded him with his fists over and over again, harder each time.

"Stop! You'll kill him!" shouted the vendor. The girls huddled together, calling for help. Now people were running towards the fray. "A fight! A fight!" The crowd expanded. Others joined in the battle and soon everyone was embroiled.

"Fetch security!" someone bellowed.

Chairs crashed to the ground. Scarves flew into the air like exotic birds. Lin had forgotten who he was fighting and why. Then he heard her voice. "Go!" He felt her hands on him. "Hurry! Run for the mountains."

Lin punched his way out of the fracas and went. People were running towards him. "What's happening?" they asked him.

He didn't answer, just kept going, as fast as he could, out of the market and the town. When he saw a road, he followed it. In front of him lay open country and yellow fields. Once again, he was a man with no home and no belongings.

9

Mei got out of the car and surveyed the apartment high-rises in front of her. The night was dark. Snow fell, fast and heavy. Once again she checked the address, confused. She had expected Kaili to live in a walled compound guarded by uniformed security staff. Instead, she found herself in a middle-class neighbourhood, with few amenities.

Mei took the lift to the twelfth floor of Building No. 4. The corridor smelled of mildew, cooking and babies. She found the right door and opened it with the key Mr Peng had given her. The corridor lights cast her shadow into the dark apartment.

She switched on the lights. The walls were covered with life-size photographs of Kaili. The apartment was silent, which heightened Mei's awareness. Her ears strained to catch the softest sound, her eyes for the slightest movement. Her heart beat almost too fast for her to breathe and her body tensed. Carefully she moved down a shadowy passage towards the bedrooms. On the walls, more pictures of Kaili mocked, but lured her on. Each closed door hid danger. At every step her fear intensified. The passage seemed to be narrowing, the walls closing in.

She was close. The door at the end swung open and a figure ran out.

Mei's head hit the wall, her sight blurred and her ears buzzed. As she slumped to the floor, she reached out a hand and caught something. There was a sharp scream and the figure fell. Mei threw herself on top and they fought. A long scratch seemed to set Mei's face on fire and a sharp elbow plunged into her chest. She gasped for air but hung on to her captive.

Eventually they stopped struggling and sat on the floor, panting.

"What are you doing here?" Mei gasped.

Miss Pink's perfectly pinned-up hair had fallen down. Her makeup was smudged.

The girl stared at Mei with loathing. "None of your business."

Mei got up. "It's Mr Peng's business." She extended a hand to Miss Pink, who took it and scrambled to her feet.

"Look what you've done to my suit!" She peered at a rip in the skirt.

When Mei had fallen, she now saw, she had caught the strap of Miss Pink's handbag. She was still holding it. Miss Pink saw it and leaped at it. But Mei was quicker. She went into the sitting room and tipped the contents on to a table: lipsticks, keys, makeup, a wallet, a pink diary, a few pens, a cigarette lighter, a packet of Virginia Slims and some letters fell on to the glass surface.

Mei grabbed them. "What have we here?"

Miss Pink bit her lip. She sat down, still catching her breath. "I don't have to tell you anything."

Mei picked up a key from the table. It was the same as the one Mr Peng had given her. "Where did you get this?"

Miss Pink reached for her cigarettes, took one out of the packet and lit it. "It's mine."

"What are you talking about?"

"This apartment's mine. He bought it for me."

She took a long puff. "He used to give me all kinds of presents, gold jewellery, pearls. He loves pearls on his women. One day he said he'd bought me an apartment. But then he met Kaili. He likes ordinary places. They don't draw attention to him. Don't you think this is the perfect hideaway for a mistress? And he's cheap – no matter how much money he has, he can't resist a bargain. Maybe that was how he found Kaili – an old shoe that had been worn too many times. She came at a discount." Miss Pink gave a nasty chuckle. A whiff of smoke leaped from her pillowy lips.

"Do you think I was stupid to think he and I shared something special? I knew he wouldn't be faithful. But I didn't mind. Look at me – I can't afford to be choosy, can I? I came to the Guanghua Record Company straight from secretarial college. We worked late at the office. We went through crises together. He said he could never have done it without me. That's the truth."

"But if Mr Peng had given this apartment to Kaili, why do you have a key?"

"I had a copy made, from the one he gave you." Miss Pink crossed her legs. "At first I didn't think much of the rumours. Kaili's one of those mad women, a fox spirit. Sometimes she disappears for days. Some say she holes up here, shooting up. But when you turned up at the office, I knew something was seriously wrong."

Miss Pink sighed. "I'm in love, Miss Wang. Can you imagine how much it hurts? I've written anonymous letters. I hate her. But I don't think Kaili cared much about them or if she did she didn't show it. I've never heard anyone talk about it. She might have thrown the letters away for all I knew. But if she hadn't I didn't want the police to find them."

Mei opened one and glanced through it. She was puzzled. "But this is a love letter."

"I was sorting through them when you arrived so I thought I'd take whatever was there. I was tired of reading them anyway. That woman doesn't care about anyone. She eats men and spits out the bones. I'm glad she's missing. I hope she's dead."

"You do know that if the police become involved, I'll have to tell them the truth."

"The truth?" Miss Pink gave a brittle laugh. "I hope you find it."

One by one she picked up her things and put them back, slowly and carefully, into her handbag. The cigarette must have calmed her. Once she had collected everything, she went to the door, pink heels clicking, hips swaying, and was gone without another word. She had appeared to regain her composure, but she had looked damaged, like her torn suit.

Mei went into the bedroom first, the most important room in any woman's house. A large brass bed took up most of the space. On one side there was a bedside table, and on the other a vanity unit. Nothing seemed out of order. If Miss Pink had searched this room, she had put everything back in its place.

She put on a pair of rubber gloves and opened the wardrobe. It was packed with clothes, long dresses, short skirts, jeans, fur and leather, mostly in black. There were also a few pieces of men's clothing, including a silk dressing-gown. On the bottom shelf she found shoes piled in heaps and, at the top, handbags from Chanel, Louis Vuitton and Gucci.

The vanity unit was messy. Makeup, scent bottles, cigarette packets and pill bottles were scattered over the surface. Mei checked the labels. Pain killers, sleeping pills … some were unidentified. She felt sorry for the woman who lived there.

In the bedside table none of the drawers was locked. She opened the top one and found bills, receipts, identity cards, appointment notes and bank books tossed together in a random pile. She took out the bank books and flipped through them. It seemed that Kaili had come into money only recently and there had been a few large withdrawals. Mei noted the dates and the amounts taken, then returned the bank books to the drawer. The next two drawers contained jewellery, strands of pearls and other gems, flung carelessly together inside boxes.

It seemed that the woman didn't care about anything, perhaps lived her life a day at a time.

At the end of the passage the study was more orderly, with trophies, awards, photo albums and scrapbooks inside a cupboard with glass doors. Two guitars leaned against it, music and notebooks on the floor nearby. The cupboard door was open, and a box lay on the floor in front of it. Miss Pink had been working through it when Mei had come in. Several letters had been opened and read, then discarded by the box. More love letters.

Mei picked up the box and took it to the desk. She switched on the lamp, and held up each item: a miniature porcelain cupid, a necklace made of tiny sea shells, an *ei* – a stone inscribed with a message of love – handkerchiefs, a pressed maple leaf that crumbled when she picked it up. Love tokens, probably.

She's vain, thought Mei. She treats them carelessly, mere tokens of her conquests. She wondered if Kaili ever looked at them or read a line or two from a letter. Did she remember the tender moments, or gloat? Perhaps she had kept them as a record, never revisiting them once they had gone into the box.

Now, bewildered, Mei took things out and examined them. She was trying to find something, anything, that might offer a clue. She was fascinated in some inexplicable way by Kaili. A different woman lay beneath the surface, she thought, and she needed to find her.

At last Mei reached the bottom of the box. Here, to her surprise, there were more letters, on old-fashioned writing-paper that had long been unavailable. They looked as if they hadn't been touched for some time, forgotten, perhaps — where the paper had been folded there were now deep grooves. Mei took them out, three in all, and spread them carefully on the table.

10

Lin followed the road uphill to the mountains and came to a village with an arched clay gate. It was evening and village elders sat on stools and logs smoking pipes beneath lush oak leaves. They might have been there all day. As Lin approached, they stopped chatting.

Lin smiled and moved to a large stone away from the tree's shade. He sat down. The dark wooden roof of a well caught his eye in the dying light. It looked like a shrine. The village, he saw, spread up the mountain's slopes, with mud houses and walls. An oil lamp glowed unsteadily in a window. The wind blew downhill, carrying with it the smell of cooking. Lin imagined sweet yellow *wotou* humming in a steamer, fatty meat boiling and noodles dropping into a soup pot.

A group of figures appeared at the hilltop, some with lamps. Their numbers grew with Lin's hunger. He could hear their voices, coming nearer. He thought of the Mao jacket, still folded inside his bundle. It would have been nice to have something like that now.

"There he is!" Children were running down the hill as fast as their feet would carry them. Other villagers — men and women returning from the fields or market — followed them. It seemed that everyone knew of a stranger's presence.

The mob stopped a foot away from Lin and stared, sizing him up.

"What are you doing here?" a man shouted.

"Where have you come from?" A woman raised her lamp to shine it on Lin's face.

"I'm looking for work. Do you need help with the harvest?"

"Call the headman!"

"Anyone seen him?"

"Field work is hard," said a balding man.

"I'm used to that," said Lin.

"The headman's coming!" A buzz went through the crowd, like wind across a barley field, and it parted to make way for him. He was about forty, stout with a measured gait and steady eyes. He smoked a pipe from the corner of his mouth. He seemed the kind of man who wouldn't do anything in a hurry.

"What is it?" He stopped in front of Lin, but he was looking at the villagers.

"The stranger says he wants work," said the young peasant who had been first to ask Lin a question.

"Do we know where he's from?"

"He doesn't say," the young man reported.

"Do you know his name?"

"No."

"Why didn't you ask?" The headman puffed his pipe, then asked Lin, "What's your name?"

"Lin," he answered. He liked the smell of the headman's tobacco, a rough local variety.

"I need to see your papers. We don't take just anyone who happens to pass through. Come with me."

Lin stood up. The crowd retreated.

"That's all," said the headman to them. "You can go home now. There's nothing else to look at."

Slowly the women went to the oak tree to retrieve their elders. The children were told to run home – some had to be dragged away. The headman walked up the hill at a leisurely pace, Lin and the rest following him like a swarm of bees.

A fat girl ran out of a house. Lin recognised her from the market.

"Ba, what's going on?" she called to the headman.

"Nothing. I told you not to come out. Is the dinner ready? Tell your ma I won't be long."

The fat girl didn't move. Her eyes were fixed on Lin. "Where are you taking him?"

"To the village office, of course. Go inside!"

The procession pressed on.

When Lin glanced back, the fat girl was alone on the slope, the hill falling away beneath her feet. It was too dark to see her face now, but Lin imagined it bulging with anxiety, as it had in the market.

In his mind, he heard her friend calling to him, her voice rising above the world: "Run to the mountains!"

The village office was a mud house with a yard. A long white board outside it read "Village Revolutionary Committee". The crowd dispersed and went home, except three youths who had appointed themselves sentries and remained outside.

Inside the committee house, the headman took down an oil lamp from a hook on the wall and lit it. Dark shadows floated and intertwined menacingly.

The headman sat down in a chair and pushed his pipe into the corner of his mouth. "I'm the only official here – headman, Party secretary, chairman of the Revolutionary Committee. Twin Wells – that's the name of our village – is small, with thirty or forty families, depending on how you count the relatives. We're poor. I don't receive a village official's allowance. At the end of the year I've got to turn in as much grain as the next man.

"If you behave, you can stay. These days, the People's Commune is an empty frame. Each family has to produce their grain quota. Harvest is a hard time. If you're no good, you leave. Understood? My word is law."

On the poster, Chairman Mao gazed enigmatically into the middle distance. What had he been looking at? Lin had no idea. A red *chun lian* hung on either side of the poster with couplets that read "Congratulations on Getting Rich". They must have been put up six months ago, for the last Spring Festival. The colour had faded.

"Are you in trouble with the police?"

Lin thought about it. Stowing away on a freight-train, fighting in the market – they could have him back behind bars tomorrow. "It's hard not to be, these days," he said.

"Watch yourself, young man."

"No, sir. I'm not in trouble."

"What about the wound on your head? It's new."

"It wasn't my fault."

"A good man doesn't fight."

"A good man doesn't lose."

"Where are you from?" asked the headman.

"Far away."

"Do you want to work or not?"

"I'm from the Qinghai mountains. Our ma is sick and needs money. Everyone says the pay is good here."

The headman shook his head. "You're lying – and lying rots a good man. Let me see your People's Commune membership card."

"I've lost my papers, and my bundle and money."

"Don't tell me someone stole it."

"No. I got into a fight and had to run."

"Then I must send you away," said the headman. "Harvest will be hard for many families, but we can't have someone with us we don't trust."

They came out to the yard. One of the three youths, who had been eavesdropping, raced off to spread the news.

Just then, a girl appeared.

"Ba, you can't send him away. Where will he go in the dark?" the headman's daughter panted.

"Fat Girl, don't meddle," barked her father.

And then Lin saw her friend, in a fitted pink top and wide black trousers. She had stopped at the gate, holding an oil lamp, the flame dancing and reflecting in her eyes.

"Ba, we know him from the market. He's a good man. He helped me and Xiao Hua," Fat Girl said, her words rolling out in rapid but disjointed bursts. "You know Big Head Du from the Du village, he and his friends attacked us. This man fought them off."

The headman turned to the other girl. "Is that true, Xiao Hua?"

She nodded.

"Why didn't you tell me this before?" the headman said to his daughter. "Does your mother know?"

Fat Girl took her father's arm, "Ba!"

He hesitated. "Perhaps you had both better come inside," he said at last.

The three went into the house and closed the door. A few minutes later they came out, the two girls holding hands and smiling.

"I have checked what you told me about the fight and your bundle," the headman said to Lin, "and you can stay. You'll sleep in the cowshed."

"Thank you ... May I have something to eat? I'm very hungry."

"Come to our house," said Fat Girl, excitedly. "Ma's cooked some meat. My name is Li Yun Yun. But everyone calls me Fat Girl."

"That's enough," the headman told his daughter. "Go and tell your mother to add a plate."

After dinner, the headman walked with Lin to the cowshed. He carried an oil lamp and a rolled-up quilt. The stars had come out and twinkled across the sky. They walked up to the edge of the village.

The night was cool. Lin heard leaves fluttering in the light breeze.

"I have let you stay. It doesn't mean I trust you."

"I'll make no trouble," Lin assured him.

"Keep away from Xiao Hua," warned the headman.

Inside the woods, a fox called. A half-moon shone above the trees.

The headman threw the quilt on to the hay. "We leave early in the morning."

After he had left, Lin climbed into the hay and fell into dreamless sleep. For a while his past disappeared.

11

The paper, so thin it was almost transparent, rustled as Mei unfolded it. The handwriting, almost calligraphy, was exquisite.

8 February 1989

Dear Kaili,

I've been home for two weeks now and I think of you every day. It's very cold, being Spring Festival and the season of Big Chill. It snowed the day before New Year's Eve.

Every time I come home, Grandpa is older. He moves slowly and sometimes forgets things, but he still works at my old school, West City No. 7 High School (he's been the caretaker for twenty years!). He thinks it will keep him agile and alive for years to come, but I worry. After all, he's seventy-one now and there's no one to look after him when I'm at university.

I'm glad I came back when term finished. I've bought more coal for Grandpa so that he can keep the heating on until spring. I took him to one of the new shopping centres in Beijing. We bought chun lian to hang beside our door – Grandpa was bewildered by the variety. He only shops in the hutong, our narrow alleyway neighbourhood. We bought firecrackers and paper for making paper cut-outs. Grandpa is very good at that – we have two phoenixes and an intricate lotus flower glued to our window.

We went to Fatty's house on New Year's Eve. We had dinner together and watched the Spring Festival gala on their television.

Fatty's home from the police academy for the festival. One day you will meet him. He's not fat and hasn't been since he was fourteen or fifteen. Three years of police training have made him strong and lean. He looks like an adult and is also more serious, but we are still the best of friends, even if we don't see each other for months at a time. When we meet again, we pick up where we left off.

Fatty and I went to the Miaohui in Ditan Park to buy things for the festival. Grandpa didn't want to come because he doesn't like crowds. Maybe he thought I'd have a better time on my own with Fatty. And we certainly enjoyed it. Fatty loves old Beijing snacks, so we had lotus-flower soup, fried green-bean-flour sausage, brown-sauce noodles, red-bean juice ...

Fatty didn't do well at school, and his parents were disappointed when he went to the police academy because it isn't a proper college. But he's done well there. He's joined the Party and was a model member last year. The instructors told him he has a promising future. His outlook on life has changed. He speaks of dreams and ambitions now.

I told him about you, that you are eighteen, clever, beautiful and brave. I told him about the time we went out with the fishermen. You'd never been to sea before and I'd only gone once on our research vessel. The fishing-boat was much smaller than our heavy ship loaded with scientific instruments. It bobbed about, at the mercy of the waves. It was already autumn, but the sun was warm. After the fishermen had dropped in their nets, we sat on the boat, chatting and waiting. The next thing I knew you had jumped into the water and were swimming like a fish, laughing at and taunting the young fishermen. Someone had dared you to do it.

I told Fatty that you impressed them. He thought you must be a bit mad — but from him that was a compliment. He asked to see a picture of you. I had to disappoint him.

I can't ask Grandpa to buy me a camera. We're short of money as it is. I don't want to tell him about you either. He thinks I'm too young to have a girlfriend. But I'll be twenty next summer. Sometimes I feel that no one has noticed I've grown up. Everyone still treats me as if I was a child. Fatty's parents hover over me just as they did when I came home from school with three-good awards. Big Papa Liu, the travelling barber who has lived in the hutong as long as my family, said I should have my hair cut by him, not in a fancy new salon.

"I've always cut your hair. Why not now?" he teased me.

The biggest problem, though, is with Grandpa. He sometimes spends an entire evening talking about the past, when my parents were alive. He's always talked of old times, but now I've been away and come back, he seems to live in the past more than ever. I wonder if, when I'm away, he thinks about it all the time. I don't blame him, but I want to talk about the future, about you, and I can't.

So, it was good to go to Fatty's house and watch the Spring Festival evening gala. We talked about what was to come. Fatty said that once he starts work he'll save up for a motorbike. His parents said he'll never be able to afford one, not on a policeman's salary.

"I'm not talking about a Honda or a Yamaha. I'll get an old military one," said Fatty. "We have a few at the academy. Once I'm married with a child, I can add a side seat to it."

His parents told him he was dreaming. "Nonsense! Our son has never done anything well. It's embarrassing, Old Neighbour," his mother said to Grandpa. "Your Lin is so clever."

Grandpa liked to hear that. He's proud to have raised me on his own.

I told Fatty's parents they should believe in their son. He's doing so well at the academy – who's to say he won't have a bright future? They said they'd believe it when it happened.

Parents and grandparents – they have strange ways of showing their love.

Fatty wasn't pleased with what his parents had said. He was quiet for a while, but after he'd eaten, he was his usual self. He wanted to know what the new year will bring. You see, Grandpa lived during the last emperor's time and knows the old customs.

At first, he didn't want to talk about it, but we persuaded him. "The year of the snake is not good," he said, "and this year will be even worse than a snake year usually is. Of the five types — earth, fire, wind, metal and water — the earth snake is particularly bad. There will be conflict, sharp dealings, turmoil and even war."

"But I thought snakes were wise," I said.

"People born in snake years are indeed wise. But the year of the snake has the strongest negative force of all the signs."

That put a dampener on the festival spirit until Fatty said, "Well, that means it'll be a good year for me. Don't they say chaos breeds heroes?"

"Oh, more nonsense!" exclaimed Fatty's mother and we laughed.

After the gala concert, at midnight, we went out to the hutong and set off fireworks in the snow. Everyone came out, even babies with their parents, everyone laughing, greeting each other, saying, "Good luck!" and "Congratulations on getting rich!" Oh, I love the hutong, the snow, my neighbours and the new year!

And I love you.

L

The lamplight glowed, illuminating the words. The letter had been written nine years ago when Kaili was a young adult. Perhaps "L" had been her first love, pure and innocent. Mei thought of her own love at that age. She had met Ya-ping when they were eighteen, on their first day at university, and fallen in love at twenty. She remembered meeting him under the pagoda at Weming Lake, the fragrance of the spring grass on its banks. It was a time of knowledge, learning, hope – the first kiss, the first words of love.

Mei's eyes returned to the letter. In those pages, Kaili was a different person: young, brave and full of life. Mei wanted to know more about her and about what had happened to that love. She opened the second letter.

12

Harvest is hard work, even for a man who is not trying to do twice as much as everyone else to earn his ticket home. All day, Lin worked in the fields, back bent, cutting wheat with a sickle. The peasants made it look easy, but he found the sickle soon became heavy. Sometimes when he straightened, he could see other men working nearby and the parts of the fields that had been cut. But what remained seemed endless. The sun beat down from early morning to late afternoon. It burned his skin dark brown.

At noon, the donkey cart came from the village with food and water. Sometimes it had to go on to the maize fields where the women picked the ears and put them into their baskets. Food enlivened the young peasants. They told rude jokes in front of their wives when they brought the food, chased them round the fields, laughing and sometimes earning themselves a good-natured slap.

Lin sat apart from them. They never dared to come up to him, though some were courteous: from time to time they'd toss over a joke or ask him about his travels, but they had heard of the fight in the market. A couple of times they had seen him lose his temper when he was provoked and were frightened by the wild beast that seemed to live inside him.

Sometimes his violence frightened even Lin. Suddenly fury would swell inside him – no one knew of it but himself – and when this happened, he knew he had to retreat into solitude. Once he was alone, he would calm down. The heat of the sun drained his mind, and, with the cicadas humming like the waves of the ocean, he dreamed of shade. He thought of the ancient oak trees that lined the streets of old Beijing and glimpses of his childhood flashed before him – a white ice-cream chiller on the back of a bicycle, the window of Grandpa's house, Fatty ...

The Xue family lived at the edge of Twin Wells, near the woods and the graveyard. That was why, according to Xiao Hua, the other villagers hardly ever visited them. "They say the wind from the graveyard blows down to us and it's unlucky. But that's superstition. We don't believe it, do we, Second Root?"

Xiao Hua's brother shook his head. He had a stutter so he rarely spoke.

Lin and Second Root sat on the *kang* – the bed made of mud – with their legs crossed and a low square table perched between them. Four dishes, a meat stew, scrambled eggs and two stir-fries, had been laid out on it. Also on the bed, waiting to eat, was Xiao Hua's father, half propped up among the pillows.

Daylight had softened to rosy dusk and steam rose from the table moistening the dry air.

Xiao Hua came in with a plate of *wotou*. "It's nothing special," she apologised to Lin.

"Too hot," her father grunted.

He was a small man who seemed to have shrunk from within. His skin was pale and wrinkled, while his eyes and mouth sunk into the flesh around them. He stared at the food grumpily. "So many dishes! You must think we're rich."

"Ba," Xiao Hua blushed, "we have a guest."

The old man coughed. Lin heard mucus bubble in his throat. "If you spend all our money, what will we eat later? The north-west wind?"

Second Root picked out a piece of meat and dropped it into Lin's bowl. "E-e-e-e-at," he said earnestly.

Flies circled above the food. Xiao Hua flapped at them, but they came back.

"Don't fuss," the old man told her. "Our guest isn't an official."

Xiao Hua gave her father a stare of desperation. "Eat slowly," she told Lin.

He watched her walk past a poster on the wall of two smiling boy babies and disappear behind a curtain into the kitchen.

"You must be relieved to have such a skilled daughter," Lin said to the old man. He felt obliged to make conversation, though it was clear that the other resented his presence.

"She leaves me rotting here all day. I'm old and sick." The old man coughed again. "Someone should look after me."

"It seems to me that your daughter does."

"She spends all our money, and we're so poor." He stopped to catch his breath. "I've worked hard all my life and raised my two children."

Second Root, who probably heard the same talk every day, paid no attention. He continued to slurp his dinner loudly. Another pillow and quilt, neatly folded, lay on the *kang* by the wall. Lin guessed they were Second Root's.

"A daughter has her duties," said the old man. "Fat Girl has no cause to worry. Her family has money."

Lin ducked his head and ate. He had no idea what the old man was talking about. He could only assume that he was on some plane known only to the elderly. He thought of Xiao Hua. She must have finished clearing up and sat on the small stool by the stove to eat.

Across the table, Second Root munched his third *wotou*.

Xiao Hua came in with a teapot and three cups. She poured for her father.

"Plastic cups. This is no banquet," grunted the old man.

Xiao Hua didn't look at him. She climbed on to the *kang* and closed the window behind him. It had a thin wooden frame with white paper, not glass, glued into it. Now the breeze was gone. The room felt stuffy. Xiao Hua brought a lamp to the table.

"Don't waste oil," said her father. "It isn't dark yet."

Xiao Hua went out to the kitchen. She came back, shielding a lighted straw with her palm, and lit the lamp.

The old man murmured in dismay.

"Drink your tea, Ba. Soon it will be time to sleep."

Lin and Second Root had finished. The plates were empty. "Hope you enjoyed your dinner," Xiao Hua said to Lin. "Just home cooking." She was collecting the dishes.

"It was very tasty." Lin smiled. "You cook well."

"Well, they say it's hard for even the best wife to manage if she has no rice," Xiao Hua said.

Her father coughed. "Women only know how to spend money."

"I earned it," retorted Xiao Hua.

The old man gasped for air and Xiao Hua's eyes clouded with guilt and pity. "You should rest now, Ba."

She took the plates and bowls to the kitchen, then lifted the square table off the *kang* and put it on the floor. Second Root laid his father's pillow in the corner. Xiao Hua soaked a towel in a basin of water and wiped her father's face. Second Root helped her to lay him down. The old man coughed.

Lin left the room. Dirty dishes were piled inside a wok on the stove. He picked up a piece of straw from a pile on the floor and pushed it into the dying flame. It caught fire and, from it, Lin lit a hand-rolled cigarette.

The kitchen was small and messy. Straw and logs were heaped together against the wall. A water-jar as tall as a small person stood by the door. Cabbage stank in a wooden bucket. Eggs, garlic, spring onions and corncobs were piled in a basket. A huge chopping knife lay beside the wok.

Lin smoked. Wood crackled in the stove. From the open door he could see into the dark evening, a few trees faintly visible. Beijing and hatred seemed very far away.

Xiao Hua and Second Root came in. Xiao Hua carried the washing basin and the lamp, and Second Root a bamboo tube with a lid.

"Second Root wants to go into the village. They're having cricket fights tonight," Xiao Hua said, as she put down the basin and the lamp.

Second Root took off the lid and showed Lin his cricket. "Wh-wh-wh-wh-what do you think?"

Lin held up the oil lamp. A tiny creature was sitting at the bottom of the tube. It didn't move.

"Are you sure it will fight?" asked Lin.

Second Root grinned and nodded.

"Do you want to go with him?" asked Xiao Hua.

"I'll stay and help you."

Xiao Hua smiled, her eyes gleaming. "Don't be late," she told her brother, who ran off.

Xiao Hua took two corncobs from the basket and threw them into the ashes in the stove. She filled the wok with water from the jar and washed the dishes.

There wasn't much Lin could do. He stood nearby, smoking.

"The house is so dirty," she said. "There's straw everywhere – and look at the flies. I clean but they come back. Years ago when Ba was well, he talked about building an extension. But we never had enough money. Everything's so expensive, especially when you go to town."

Her hands moved fast, like fish, flipping in and out of the water. She piled each plate or bowl with the others on the mud surface by the stove. "Have you been to a city?" she asked.

"Yes."

"Was it nice?"

"Very."

"I suppose the girls were fashionable and pretty, like you see in magazines."

"You're pretty."

"Help me with the water," said Xiao Hua.

He lifted the wok and poured the dirty water outside the house.

She dried her hands on the hem of her top. Of course she knew she was pretty   Lin looked into the big eyes, with long lashes – but it wasn't enough.

"They say a woman's beauty is thirty per cent nature and seventy per cent makeup. If only I had money," she murmured.

"You're safe and you have your family. It may not sound much to you now, but it's worth everything."

Xiao Hua took the stool outside. "Come here," she called. "It's cooler."

Lin followed her and sat on the doorstep.

"Do you miss your home?" Xiao Hua asked.

"Yes. When I finish here, I'll go back. What began there has to finish there."

"You mean you'll bring money back home?"

"Money means nothing to me. It can't buy back what I've lost."

"What happened?"

"It's a long story." Lin tried to smile. "Maybe one day I'll tell you."

Xiao Hua took a puff of his cigarette. "I'd do anything for money. I'm tired of being poor."

"There are worse things than poverty."

"Are there? This spring we ran out of food and didn't have money to buy any more for two months. Second Root and I dug roots in the woods. We had no money for Ba's medicine. If the headman hadn't lent us some yuan, Ba might have died. Second Root had no winter coat. We couldn't afford spring couplets for New Year. It was shaming! Forty miles away everyone knew about the poor Xue family."

"At least you're free."

"What good is that when you are shackled by poverty? The matchmakers offer me Idiot Du and Mad Huang. Is that all I am? A cheap bride? Ba's ashamed too, but he won't show it. He wants the money from my marriage – and I'd take anyone for Ba's sake, and Second Root's. Of course I would. They're my only flesh and blood …" Her voice tapered off.

But she couldn't, Lin thought. She couldn't give up on herself yet.

"My poor dead mother." Xiao Hua gazed towards the graveyard. In the darkness nothing moved but the stars twinkling in the sky. "I wish she was still here. We were happy once."

Lin wanted to take her hands and tell her his story. He

wanted to share with her his burden. But he stopped himself. He had to be careful. Under no condition should he let anyone know who he was.

At that moment he felt the heaviness as well as the beauty of life. The translucent night, the silvery sky, the scent of the summer breeze and the sound of wildlife on the mountains tore at his heart and made him think of another summer night on another doorstep.

"Travel a million miles
Searching everywhere
But nowhere could I find
The heart of my youth ..."

"What's that?"

"Part of a poem."

"Did you write it?"

"No. It was written by a poet who died more than a thousand years ago."

Xiao Hua stared at him. He could see she was confused, searching for answers in his face.

"Who are you? A vagrant doesn't know poetry."

"Years ago an old man taught it to me. I thought I'd forgotten it," he lied, shrugging it off. "I don't know what it means, but it sounds nice."

Xiao Hua smiled. Equilibrium had been restored. She went inside.

The corncobs were done. She took them out of the stove, dusted off the ashes and carried them out on the hem of her blouse.

Lin and Xiao Hua sat side by side on the doorstep, eating their corn. The oil lamp was burning out. Xiao Hua's breasts rose and fell beneath the cotton top, her shoulder almost touching Lin's. He could smell the scent of her skin and feel her warmth. The memory of the ocean and of the woman he had loved long ago took shape. Desire rose in him.

Mosquitoes came from the woods, whining a victory hymn.

13

28 May 1989

Dear Kaili,

I'm sorry I couldn't write sooner. I know you're worried, but don't be, my love.

It was only after I got home that I saw how worried Grandpa has been. So much has happened and is still happening in Beijing, far beyond what we had imagined.

The Street and Hutong Revolutionary Committee received a communiqué from the city and Party Central about the student movement, saying it was anti-revolutionary and warning of consequences for those who participated. The chairwoman, Mrs Tang, lives in our hutong. She went to see Grandpa and upset him so much that he panicked and telegraphed me.

When I got home, he told me, "It's less worrying if you're here. Than I can make sure you don't get into trouble."

The students weren't causing trouble, I said. They wanted only democracy and freedom so that every Chinese could live a better life.

Grandpa said he didn't understand democracy and freedom, but he knew what a good life was — one without trouble, turmoil or death. "You'll be happy if you don't expect too much of life. And it's never worth challenging the Communist Party."

I can't blame him. He lost his only son to the Cultural Revolution.

But I told him things would be different this time. China has moved into a modern time and opened to the world. Chairman Mao has been dead for almost thirteen years and the Party has re-evaluated his legacy.

People of our parents' generation talk about being Red Guards during the Cultural Revolution, how exciting that time was — until the revolution turned to mass destruction. On the train to Beijing, I felt for the first time that I understood the thrill of hope. The other passengers shared their food with us and said how much they appreciated what the students were doing for the country. Many of us were allowed on to the train without tickets, an act of support by the guards and ticket salesmen.

The mood in Beijing was more guarded. Yesterday I went to Tiananmen Square, but I couldn't get inside the student security zone even with my university identification card. I saw students turning away supporters from factories or provincial universities. They seemed tense. One told me they were afraid of secret police infiltrating the square.

They had stopped their hunger-strike, but thousands still sat in the square. University flags still flew. The loudspeakers still broadcast denunciations of the Party's treatment of students. But there was no sense of purpose. Now that the government had survived the hunger-strike and demonstrations a million strong, no one harboured any illusion that it would give in. The students didn't want to retreat but there seemed no chance that they would win. Visitors still put money into the collection boxes and wondered what it was for. There was an impasse in the square and no one could see the end.

Many students who had come from all over the country wandered around the streets. They were unhappy that the Beijing students hadn't welcomed them. Many had travelled for days to be here. The Beijing students were worn out, but the newcomers were still enthusiastic and full of energy. They talked about organising themselves. They felt they had missed the action.

In Qingdao we felt left out, didn't we? Of course we went to the city hall to demonstrate our support for the hunger-strikers. We scuffled with the police. We went to the station and lay on the tracks to stop trains carrying military supplies to Beijing — but who knew what they were carrying or where they were going? We did those things because we felt we must and because, deep down, we felt guilty that we were not in Beijing, standing shoulder to shoulder with our fellows. There had even been talk of a hunger-strike of our own, but the number of volunteers was small. Everyone wanted to be in Beijing.

I was speaking the truth when I told you I didn't want to leave you but I had to come back for Grandpa's sake. I wish you could have come with me.

I haven't found it easy to be at home because I am not at a Beijing university. I couldn't get into Tiananmen Square or join the student anti-tank blockages on the outskirts of the city. I tried to contact my old highschool friends, now at Beijing University, but I couldn't find anyone. Everyone was on the streets.

Today we heard that soldiers had been seen in the city centre, albeit only a platoon. Grandpa won't let me go out at night now. The evenings have been warm. After dinner, neighbours come out to chat or walk together round the neighbourhood, in the narrow alleyways. Everyone is worried about what might happen next.

I'm anxious too, although I don't believe many of the things Grandpa and our neighbours have said. But I do wonder whether our youth has made us over-optimistic. We all know what happened in the Cultural Revolution and how brutally people's lives were crushed. I lost my mother and father in that violence. Yet we discount history. We hope too much. We dream of our own greatness. Imagine that the students win. What will we do? Can we run a government? Can we rebuild China? We are only twenty. Revolution is one thing, production another.

I hope you're not frustrated by my pessimism, as you called it. I remember you getting impatient when we discussed it. You said I was making difficult when there was none. You said I was going through the senior-year-at-university phase, mistaking disbelief for maturity.

You never doubted. You believed in life, love and, most of all, hope. Being with you was like bathing in sunlight, enough to make me think of abandoning my inner demon. But I have one and it leers at me during the night. I tremble with fear, and I don't know why.

I wish you were here. You would give me courage. The sparkle in your eyes would lighten my darkest thoughts.

I think of the night we spent in your room. Revolution is good – no one cares about rules now. Somewhere a demonstration was taking place and your roommates had gone to it. There must have been stars outside the window and the world was in ferment around us, faith collapsing, fires burning. But none of that mattered.

You know I love you, don't you? I shall love you till the end of my days.

Grandpa is snoring at the other end of the room, his wrinkled face as peaceful as a child's. Soon I'll tell him about you, our plan to marry and stay in Qingdao after we graduate. He will be heartbroken. But it's for the best. We belong by the sea.

I hope the mail trains are running and that you receive this letter. I don't know when I'll see you again, but I'm counting the days, hours and minutes.

Love,

L

Mei put down the letter. She was breathing fast. Kaili and her lover had been involved in the student movement, which Mei had witnessed and, to her regret, taken no part in.

Now she felt a connection with them. She recognised the passion that had been theirs pounding in her own heart. They were her contemporaries. They had shared history.

Mei felt drawn to L in particular, perhaps because he was from Beijing and closer to her in age, or perhaps because she was reading his words in his own handwriting. In her mind she pictured him, pale with short black hair and gentle eyes, a book in his hand, quiet and thoughtful. But he was brave too.

What had happened to him? What had happened to their love? Mei wanted to know. With trembling hands, she picked up the last letter.

3 June 1989

Dear Kaili,

The evening is deepening and the hutong *is quiet. I am waiting for Grandpa to go to sleep. He is lying in his bed three feet from me, at the other end of the room, still stirring. The heat has cooled, so hopefully he will soon be asleep.*

I want to write to you before I go.

Grandpa has forbidden me to go out at night. We live not far from the city centre. If I take my bicycle, I could be in Tiananmen Square or Changan Boulevard in half an hour. Out there, thousands of my contemporaries are making history. But I sit here evening after evening, with a group of older men, and sometimes older women, listening to them talk about the past.

I long to go out!

Grandpa lets me go where I like during the day. Every morning I get up early and leave the hutong. *I want to know what happened overnight and to be with people my own age.*

The situation in Beijing is desperate now. Fear has set in. Buses were burned to make roadblocks on Changan Boulevard. Trucks and cars have been seized and heaped together. No one doubts now that the army will be sent in. The students are preparing for the clash. Everyone is talking about tear gas and rubber bullets.

How did we get to this point? I don't know. The city looks like a war zone.

I meet people on the streets, mostly students from the provinces. Some are staying with relatives, but others have wandered the streets since they arrived and sleep rough. They float on the periphery, like fallen leaves. They want to play their part. They sense history being made. I'm like them, in trying to find out what's happening, but I don't share their restlessness and näivety.

I know what you would say — that I'm being pessimistic again. Perhaps. But do you think we've thought everything through? When the students drafted their demands, did they consider how likely it was that they would be met? When they went to Tiananmen Square for the hunger-strike, did they believe it would make a difference — that the mighty Chinese Communist Party would surrender because a few students might kill themselves?

I'm speaking not as a man who lost his parents in one of Mao's political movements but as a detached analyst of history. Death has always come cheaply to the Chinese, not just in the People's Republic — millions in the Great Leap Forward and hundreds of thousands in the Cultural Revolution — but under generations of emperors.

If we try to change the course of history with blood, we must be prepared to see it run in rivers. But bloodshed and death are not the way forward. There has already been too much of both.

Somehow I feel death near, in the air. Maybe the mosquito coil is making me dizzy — or the night; it's stuffy and too quiet. I'm angry because I'm afraid.

I'm reminded now of another incident. Around lunchtime, a group of students from the provinces and I were sitting on a kerb. The streets were mostly deserted, no buses or cars. Every now and then, people cycled past. We were discussing where we might go to find action.

Then about a dozen students rode past — a red flag with "Beijing Space College" streamed behind one of their bicycles. Some of the group wore white headbands. I couldn't read what was written on them, they were going towards Tiananmen Square.

Everyone cheered, and one punched the air, shouting, "Fight till the end!"

Our spirits rose. The sun was shining and the wide boulevard radiated heat. We watched them disappear.

My companions began to talk about death. One was just eighteen. She said she would die to wake people like her parents to reality. It was as though our country was dead. How, she asked, could people submit themselves without question to the iron rule of the Party?

I couldn't bear to listen any longer, so I left.

She reminded me of you. I remembered the night we spent at Qingdao station. We sat while some of our fellow students lay down on the tracks so that the trains couldn't move. Your eyes shone with innocence and excitement. You insisted on sitting directly in front of the engine.

There were perhaps a hundred people at the station and we sang all night, old Soviet and folk songs, revolutionary hymns, lullabies, rock'n'roll anthems. We felt as though we belonged to a divine plan and that our lives had a higher purpose. We were so frightened that we couldn't keep quiet for a minute.

I felt the same fear on the streets of Beijing, but there no one sang. In the shadow of ancient palaces, we were quiet. In our silence we could almost hear catastrophe.

Yet we tried to defy it. The more hopeless the situation, the more we wanted to fight. Perhaps we had hoped that through bravery we could repel this horrible feeling of demise.

The eighteen-year-old girl had puffy cheeks. She said that we would inflict the greatest tragedy on our country by not trying to change things. Do you agree? Will we regret it one day if we don't fight till the end?

This evening, the radio has broadcast warnings from the city government. It is urging citizens and students not to go out tonight. Of course, when I said that I wanted to find out what was going on, Grandpa refused point-blank to allow it.

To him, there is no doubt of what will happen tonight. The army, which has massed outside Beijing, will march in.

The mosquito coil has burned out. Grandpa has not stirred for a while. Perhaps he's asleep at last.

I will wait for another five minutes, to be sure. Then I will go out of the hutong, cycle down South Drum Tower Street to Tiananmen Square. I've stayed at home too long, whether from cowardice or intellect I don't know. I must go out. It's the only way to find out what has been going on.

I think of those students lying in front of the tanks at the West Mountains. I compare myself with them. They have something I lack. They are determined. They don't question or hesitate. I envy them.

Now I'm away, I think more of you than ever. I run your features through my mind like a film. I see your eyes lighting up and your face shining with a kind of beauty that is as clear as a child's heart. I wonder what makes you so radiant. It's more than youth. It's passion and faith.

It seems depraved to think of love when Death lurks in the shadows. But talk of ideals has dried me out. The thought of you, like cool water, gives me courage. I love you.

There is an old maple tree in our hutong. When I was little, I used to climb it and sit on one of its high branches to watch dusk fall on the Drum Tower. Grandpa told me that, in imperial times, twenty-four drums would beat to mark the hour and the changing of the night watches. Perhaps for that reason I always felt the tower, with its layered butterfly roofs and thick walls, had a mystical power.

At the top of the maple, I could also see the hutong, *its narrow alleys winding this way and that, like a maze, like the roots of an ancient tree. Each year the roots grew a little. More people moved into the courtyards, babies were born, children married. Somewhere a wall decayed and a house crumbled, or an extension was built in whatever space could be found; pigeon lofts went up; roofs were mended. Like an ugly but indestructible primitive life form, the* hutong *lived on.*

Perhaps this is how it will end. I hope life, not death, triumphs.

I have to go. But I promise I will write again very soon. Yours for ever,

L

The pages slipped out of her fingers. Mei remembered that night in Tiananmen Square. From the ministry's residential compound, where she lived, she heard tanks and other army vehicles rumbling down Changan Boulevard and ran out to see what was happening. A stray bullet flew past her and her roommate. Artillery lit up the dark sky. The mighty machine of the Chinese Army had come to crush unarmed students. She remembered writing to Ya-ping, her boyfriend studying in Chicago, to let him know that some of their friends had been wounded, others were missing. She wrote several long letters about what she had seen that night and in the days that followed. She wrote about her guilt at not having been in the square, and her loneliness. She felt her friends had abandoned her, as she had abandoned them when they needed her. She felt guilty for having been unable to help.

Mei had never posted those letters, knowing that they would be read by the state security machine. Ya-ping didn't write then either. Mei thought perhaps he feared the same repercussions. But when she heard from him a few months later, he told her he had fallen in love and would not be coming back.

Now Mei felt a crunching thirst. Light-headed, she got up and went into the kitchen. In the years that had followed, she had wondered whether Tiananmen Square had played a part in Ya-ping's decision.

The fridge was almost empty, but for a few cans of beer and a bottle of sake. Mei drank some tap water, hoping she wouldn't be ill the next day.

On her way back to the study, she heard a noise outside the apartment. Her heart skipped a beat. What if someone found her? What could she say or do to defend herself? She stood still and strained her ears to listen. Someone was talking loudly in the corridor. It sounded like a dispute between neighbours.

The evening had deepened, and Mei looked at her watch. It was approaching eleven o'clock. She took a deep breath and tried to clear her thoughts. She was transfixed by what she had read. What had happened to L? Did he and Kaili ever meet again? Had he died in the square? She wanted to find out more about him and about the Kaili no one seemed to know.

She searched through albums and scrapbooks. There were publicity photos and pictures taken at parties but nothing "old", no childhood pictures. She went on leafing through the pages, becoming more and more frustrated. Then she stopped. A paper butterfly was pasted to the first page of a scrapbook. Carefully she detached it and held it up to the light. It was made from white rice paper so sheer it was almost transparent. The wings were shaped around hair-thin bamboo frames and painted with golden veins. When Mei turned it, the butterfly appeared to flutter its wings. Then she saw, with a jolt, a small golden "L" inscribed on one.

14

Xiao Hua set the basket beside her mother's grave. She pulled out some grass and smoothed the soil. The headstone was small and bore no inscription. Over time it had eroded and cracked. From the basket she took out a bowl of steamed buns and another of apples, then placed them in front of the headstone. "Come, Second Root. Give Ma a *ketou*."

Second Root knelt beside his sister. They bowed.

"Harvest was good this year, Ma. We bought a new course of herbs for Ba. He said maybe we could even put away a little money for Second Root. It's time for him to take a bride."

"N-n-n-n-n-no."

"You'll soon be eighteen. It's time." Xiao Hua gave her brother a gentle look. She turned to the stone again and put her palms together. "Ma, this is Lin. He's the man I've been telling you about. Without his help we wouldn't have done so well this harvest. We've been lucky, Ma. Thank you for watching over us."

Xiao Hua and Second Root got up. They took scraps of white ghost money from the basket and lit it. The flame grew slowly and dark smoke swirled, then fire engulfed the paper, sending sparks into the wind.

When it had gone out, leaving only ash and thin smoke, Lin bade them farewell.

"G-g-g-goodbye, older brother." Second Root held out his hand, and Lin shook it.

"Second Root," he said, "you're clever. Don't let anyone say otherwise."

Second Root pressed his lips together and nodded. He seemed to want to say more but no words came. He just smiled.

Xiao Hua gave Lin a small packet, wrapped in a piece of cloth cut from a length she had bought. "Don't open it yet."

But Lin ignored her. Inside, he found a pair of new straw shoes and some money folded into a square. "I can't take this. It's your savings." There were no more than five or six notes, but he knew what they meant to the Xue family.

Xiao Hua pushed the money back into his hands. She was crying now. "Go! Go now!"

"Goodbye," said Lin. He knew, somehow, they would never meet again.

He turned and walked down the mountain, his footsteps unsteady. He didn't look back. At the foot, he searched for the road that would take him home.

PART TWO

15

Mei didn't sleep well. Fragments of Lin's letters penetrated her dreams. She woke dazed the next morning, and sat in bed for some time, thinking about the past.

She had been working at the Ministry for Public Security in the spring of 1989, which had begun like any other spring. Weeping willows turned green, lilies bloomed on riverbanks. After the long, cold winter, families went to the West Mountains for the Festival of Peach Blossom.

But as the weather grew warmer and the magnolias filled the emperor's courtyard at the Summer Palace with snowy flowers, she felt restless. She waited anxiously for letters from Ya-ping, her boyfriend of three years who had moved to America the previous summer. They arrived less and less often.

April 15 was warm. She remembered it because that was the day on which she had telephoned Ya-ping. She had gone to the Friendship Hotel, one of the few places in Beijing from which international calls could be made, and spent her monthly pay on the telephone. She had sat in the booth with tears rolling down her cheeks, overwhelmed with joy to hear his voice. Graduate school had turned out to be more difficult than he thought, he said, and he had to go to extra language classes, but he promised to write soon. "I love you," he said in English, before they hung up.

On 15 April that year the former Communist Party chairman, Hu Yaobang, had died of a heart-attack. The news had surprised everyone. The ministry had buzzed with agents for days afterwards. Mei had been at the end of her year-long induction programme, working overtime in the PR head's office. Her boss, who later asked her to become his personal assistant, had begun to hint at a bright future for her in the ministry.

Then there had been trouble. Many university students had seen Hu Yaobang as their sympathiser and protector, for he had been tolerant of student protests during his chairmanship, and demanded to attend his funeral. But he had also been the head of China's ruling party so his funeral was a state affair. The students were not invited.

On the day, the ministry was tense. Reports that students were sitting in protest outside the Great Hall of the People had spread like wildfire. People slid from one office to another trying to find out what was happening. Mei heard that twenty thousand students were sitting in Tiananmen Square.

After work she went to see some friends, a young couple who lived in her block. The three sat in front of the television with a meal from the ministry canteen and watched the day's events.

In the early morning, forty thousand students had gathered in a sit-down protest on the west side of Tiananmen Square. They chanted slogans and sang. Red flags represented almost every higher-education institution in Beijing. Inside the Great Hall of the People, the funeral continued as planned. All of the top officials were in attendance.

Outside, the sun shone. There was a commotion. A side door opened and some staff of the Great Hall emerged. Student representatives went to meet them, taking with them a petition bearing ten thousand signatures. They wanted to deliver it to the government. The staff told the students they were disruptive and asked them to leave.

After they had disappeared back into the Great Hall, the students returned to their comrades. A little later, three walked out of the crowd and up the imposing stone steps. They stopped at the top and knelt down, holding the petition above their heads.

Mei and her friends were silent. The reporter said they had stayed where they were for forty minutes, but no one had come to receive the scroll.

That night, lying on her pillow, Mei saw those images again in her mind's eye: the faces of students who seemed familiar, faces as young as her own, the sun radiating on the red flags, the three figures kneeling on the stone steps. Her heart ached.

Within days, students were walking out of classrooms. They marched into the streets and went to Tiananmen Square.

There, they demanded freedom of speech and democracy. A federation of university students was established and a delegation formed to instigate dialogue with the government. Soon, workers, government employees, parents and grandparents had joined in.

Meetings were held daily in the ministry and everyone was told that the testing time had come. Their future would be determined by their choice: would they side with the People and the Party or with the anarchists? "It is in crisis that one's true conviction is revealed," the minister shouted into a microphone.

But Mei's thoughts were in the streets and in Tiananmen Square. She imagined her friends marching, calling for freedom and democracy. She wanted to escape the high walls of the Ministry for Public Security.

Mei met Big Sister Hui at a street-corner café in *zhongguancun*, near their alma mater Peking University. When Mei had left the university, Big Sister Hui had stayed on to do a master's degree.

"Don't come, Mei," Big Sister Hui warned, over a tin of coconut milk. "Whether you like it or not, if you join the students, you will be seen as representing the Ministry of Public Security. Some will consider you a heroine but others may suspect you of infiltrating our movement. Are you sure you want to be a heroine? I certainly don't want to be caught up in a spy scandal. Besides, we have plenty of supporters. One more won't make any difference." Her voice sounded mocking.

"What do you mean?"

"Mei, you're my friend. When you asked me to meet you here, I came, even though I'm very busy. Fifty of our students, most of them eighteen or nineteen, are on hunger-strike in Tiananmen Square. So I'll be frank. You aren't made for heroics, and you're a loner – the very idea of joining a collective action, which ours is, would probably make you sick."

"Are you saying I'm a coward?"

"No! Just that you're not a follower. The very fact that you want to talk to me instead of running to the street with a banner, saying, "Police Support Students" says much about you. You've never been comfortable with mass movements. One day you'll be braver than all of us, but you'll do it in your own way."

A truck packed with students drove past. A red flag flew from it, illuminated with four glorious characters: *Bei Jing De Xue* – Peking University. Pedestrians waved and shouted in support. Cyclists rang their bells.

Big Sister Hui's eyes shone. "This time we have a good chance of winning. For days, a million people have been marching round Tiananmen Square supporting the hunger-strike – perhaps the whole country has mobilised. When I was there yesterday, I really felt it was the will of the People. Everywhere you looked there was a sea of faces, red flags and banners.

"I'm sure you know that communiqués have been pouring down from Party Central. In one it was said that the students were being misled by anti-revolutionaries, and another called for each Party member to abide by the Party line. How do I know? Oh, Mei, we have our sources. My parents are frightened. They saw so much horror in the Cultural Revolution. My father still bears the scars of his labour-camp days. Even now his knee hurts when it rains. But it was your father who died in prison."

Mei lowered her eyes. Her coffee had gone cold but she drank it anyway. It tasted bitter.

But Big Sister Hui was wrong about victory. It had taken only one night for the army to clear Tiananmen Square. Thousands lay dead or injured in the hospitals near Changan Boulevard. Beijing came under martial law.

Two days later, Mei tried to cycle to the city centre. Normally crowded and noisy, it was remarkably silent. There were no bicycle bells or children's cries. The colour seemed to have drained out too. Burned vehicles, shattered bricks, blackened bloodstains and debris from the fighting littered the streets. There were no more red flags or eager young faces with white headbands. Bullet holes pocked the walls of apartment buildings. Soldiers, their semi-automatics ready to fire, guarded road crossings.

Mei was stopped at an intersection. A long line of covered army trucks thundered down the boulevard, gun barrels poking out from the sides. Fear chilled her to the bone. She never reached the city centre. It had been closed off.

Within days, most of the student leaders had been arrested and were sentenced later to lengthy prison terms. The movement's "hooligans" and "bad elements" were executed. Mei waited for Ya-ping's letters, which never came.

The radiator next to her bed clunked, rousing Mei from the past. She got up, put on a heavy cardigan over her pyjamas and went to the window. The rooftops of Beijing rambled under hazy sky to the horizon.

The army had marched into Beijing and opened fire on the students on 4 June 1989. Over the past nine years, this date had become a secret. The government never mentioned it, but Tiananmen Square was closed each year on the anniversary. No one talked about it. It was as if a chest had been buried underground and the key thrown away. But every so often something happened and memories as fresh as the emotions of that day soared inside Mei. This time it had been L's letters.

Mei made a cup of coffee and sat down with it on the sofa. She had gone to Kaili's apartment looking for answers, but had come away with more questions. She didn't know whether they would bring her closer to finding Kaili. Yet she was encouraged. She had discovered truth, and however small and distant it might be, it would lead her to more. She picked up the paper butterfly that lay beside L's letters on the coffee-table. She wondered at its beauty and the meaning it might hold.

The drive to her office was stressful. As soon as Mei came off the ring road, she was stuck in a traffic jam that went on for miles. Cyclists swerved through the stationary cars and trucks, often crashing into each other. Buses ground black smoke and dirt into the snow. Shops at the roadside remained shut, but gaudy advertisements remained to taunt passers-by from the windows.

When Mei finally turned into her office car park, snow had covered the old oak tree. It stood like an elaborate sculpture, as if someone had iced each of its branches with pristine white sugar, a monument to renewal. Mei turned off the engine. She glanced up at the last window on the first floor, where a row of icicles hung, and wondered whether Gupin was in.

At the door bicycles, wheels chained, were stacked against each other. A small man stood next to them, huddled under a winter jacket and a padded army hat with ear-flaps. His back was bent. His limbs seemed to have retracted into his body. From time to time he stamped his feet and blew into his gloved hands. Mei stole a look at him as she went past. Two beady eyes peered out from beneath the hat, moved rapidly, then stopped to stare at her.

She slipped into the building.

"Take your hot water up!" shouted the caretaker.

His door was ajar. Mei pushed it open and saw him sitting at the window gazing out, his legs propped on the table. He was listening to Beijing opera on an old-fashioned radio and singing along, off-key, his head swaying. Suddenly he slapped his thigh. On the radio, the male character had stretched a high note into a thin cry. As if tracing its ascent, the caretaker reached with his right hand, trembling, towards the ceiling.

Mei picked up a hot-water Thermos and called, "Thank you!" The caretaker didn't turn, but he waved to acknowledge that he had heard her.

In her office, everything was as she had left it. No sign of

Gupin. Mei closed the door. Gupin's computer stood, a lonely reminder of him, on his desk in the anteroom. There were no messages on the answering-machine.

She heard a a soft, almost timid tap at the door. Half a minute later, there was another.

Mei opened the door. The small man she had seen at the entrance to the building was standing in front of her. He still wore the army hat with ear-flaps but his back had straightened. The light coming through the door shone on him. His face was young, almost mischievous.

"Are you Wang Mei?" he asked, in a heavy accent.

"Yes?"

"I'm Gupin's friend. People call me Little Mountain."

"I'm afraid Gupin's not here," Mei said, still holding the door.

"I know. That's why I came. He had an accident yesterday and was taken to hospital."

"Come in."

Little Mountain stepped into the room. He took off his hat and twisted it between his fingers.

"Where is he? Which hospital?" asked Mei, her heart drumming.

"He's at home now. He can't stay in hospital – we aren't allowed medical care."

Of course, Mei thought. Migrant workers don't receive benefits in Beijing. "How is he?" She asked.

"He has some cuts and a broken leg."

"Won't you sit down?" Mei pulled out a chair.

"No, thank you. I came to ask for help. Gupin's not well. He has a fever. Do you know a doctor who will visit him? We can pay cash."

"A doctor!" Mei thought of Lu, who probably had the best contacts in the city. "Please wait," she said to Little Mountain. She went into her office and picked up the phone.

"It's you!" her sister exclaimed. She was in her dressing room getting ready for her show. "I thought it would be that incompetent estate agent again. I'm trying to buy some flats as an investment. Property prices are rising but so are rents."

Mei told her what had happened to Gupin.

"Of course, I know doctors and chief surgeons," said Lu, "but I don't think they'd want to go treat a migrant worker, especially in this weather. Can't he find a doctor for himself? Mei, he's taking an advantage of you. This isn't your problem. I never liked you employing a migrant worker – there was sure to be trouble."

"I must help him. He's my assistant." He was her friend too and she wouldn't let him down.

"Maybe it's time to find another. Listen to me, sister, you're too kind-hearted. It's not up to you to look after Gupin. He's just an employee."

Mei hung up, disappointed. She sat behind her desk and thought for a while. Perhaps her childhood friend, Ding, would help? He used to be a doctor, but two years ago he had left the hospital to make more money selling medical equipment. Mei thought it a waste for a graduate of China's top medical school to make a living as a travelling salesman.

She dialled his number. He and his wife lived in her apartment block. There was a communal phone on each floor.

To Mei's surprise, it was Ding who answered. "You are not away?" she asked.

"The government's cracking down again." Ding seemed not to care who might hear him. Mei guessed that everyone else had gone to work. "It's Spring Festival. You know how it likes to tighten control during the 'special period'. Hospitals have to abide by the rules and get all they need from the Bureau for Medical Equipment."

"Does that mean you're not busy?"

"It does. I'll be back at work in a month's time when it's all blown over."

"Could you come out to treat a friend? My assistant was hurt in a traffic accident. He's from the provinces and doesn't have medical insurance in Beijing. But he can pay cash – though perhaps not much."

"Don't worry about the money. Where is he?"

Mei was embarrassed that she didn't know. "Where does Gupin live?" she asked Little Mountain.

"South Pound Village."

"Where's that?"

"Near Seven Trees."

"Ding, do you know Seven Trees?"

"Yes, but it'll take me a while to get there. There isn't a direct bus from where I am."

"Get a taxi. I'll pay. Ask the driver to go to South Pound Village. I'll see you there."

They hung up.

"Where's Seven Trees?" asked Mei, putting on her coat.

"Near Half-a-Shop," said Little Mountain.

"Can you direct me?"

"I think so."

16

Little Mountain wasn't very good at giving directions. He didn't know any of the street names. They looked for landmarks he had seen from buses and got lost a couple of times, but eventually they were in Seven Trees. Mei drove down the main street, then made a sharp turn. Soon they were driving down a country lane. On both sides, snow-covered fields stretched out like wasteland. Mei's little red Mitsubishi struggled on the icy road, the engine threatening to stall. Through the windscreen, she could just make out a village on the horizon.

Little Mountain talked ceaselessly. "My wife works at a restaurant. They have a phone. Someone from the hospital called her, perhaps a nurse. Normally her boss doesn't let anyone leave early, even when they're not busy, but at the moment my wife is in his good books because we stayed in Beijing to work through the festival. They need help for the holiday. It's big-money time. We have a son, a year old. He's with his grandparents. When he's older, we'll bring him to Beijing. We don't want to go home. Life's good here."

"How was Gupin when he got to hospital?" Mei was anxious to find out more about what had happened.

"First, my wife came to find me. I asked our foreman if I could have the rest of the day off, but he said no, we'd all come in late. Well, we couldn't help that – there was a snow storm. He said he wasn't paying us to be late. He said construction waits for no one. The turtle's egg! We haven't been paid in months!

"He shouted when I left, telling me I shouldn't bother to come back. Dog! I'm not afraid of him. Most migrant workers go home for Spring Festival, and there's plenty of work. You go to the pick-up areas in the morning and you get something straight away."

"How did Gupin look when you saw him?"

"When my wife and I got there, he was lying on a bed in the emergency room, all bandaged up. They'd operated and put a cast on his leg. The doctor said they couldn't give him a bed but he should be looked after, and gave him some painkillers. I borrowed a flat-bed cart from a brother who works near the hospital and we took Gupin home. The storm was bad. I pedalled the cart twenty-five *li*, all the way to South Pound. On the way, my wife said she wanted to make chicken soup for Gupin. But with the blizzard, where could she get a chicken?"

Just then, they arrived at the edge of the village. Mei stopped the car beside a wooden bridge and they got out. The temperature had fallen even lower, and the wind chilled their bones. They walked across the bridge, which creaked under their feet. Beneath, a frozen stream was covered with snow.

"Gupin is like a brother to me," said Little Mountain. "Last winter when I was injured at work he helped to pay my medical bills and took care of my wife and son. He has a heart of gold." He nodded vigorously.

An alleyway about two metres wide wound through tightly packed courtyard houses. The walls were cracked, and the plaster peeling in places to expose rotten bricks. On the ground there were yellow patches of ice littered with frozen cabbage leaves and little bones. Mei and Little Mountain passed the public lavatory and a leafless tree.

An old man emerged from one of the courtyards, coughing, his thin grey hair blowing in the wind. Behind him, the wooden gate creaked shut. It was plastered with notices warning of "sexual diseases".

"Here we are," said Little Mountain, pushing it open again.

Mei followed him. As she stepped through, doubt rose in her mind. Little Mountain disappeared into a grey house across the courtyard. It was slightly bigger than its neighbours, the windows taped shut and covered with newspaper.

Mei stopped. The newspapers were forever printing stories of kidnappings and robberies in such places. The ancient walls, crumbling since the days of the emperors, seemed to close in on her.

The door opened again and Little Mountain reappeared, beckoning her over. Mei drew a deep breath. She had come this far. All she had to do now was walk the last few steps.

The room smelled of smoke from a coal stove. Gupin was sitting up in bed, propped against two pillows. His face was distorted by cuts, bruises and large sticking plasters. One of his hands was bandaged. A quilt covered his legs but one was clearly bigger than the other. "Little Mountain shouldn't have brought you here," he said. He was smiling, but Mei could see he was ill. His eyes were dull, his face feverish.

"I wanted to come. How are you feeling?" She went to him and sat by his side on the edge of the bed. "Little Mountain told me all about it. A doctor friend of mine is coming to see you."

She cast a glance round the room. It was simply furnished. A water-jar stood by the door with a calabash, hollowed out for use as a ladle, balanced on its lid. A cabinet stood against the wall, rolled-up quilts and two cardboard boxes piled on top. A washing-line hung across the room, cutting a triangle from the stove to Gupin's bed. Two hand towels were drying on it. A pile of coal stood by the stove.

"It's dirty," said Gupin, panting.

Little Mountain interrupted: he was going out, he said, but would be back soon.

"Why do you live here?" Mei asked, puzzled. "I pay you well. You could have rented a room, if not an apartment, in the city."

Gupin eyed the dirty window and a hole in the wall that had been filled with newspaper. "It's cheap here. The more I save, the more I can send home to my mother. She's paralysed, so she's always short of money. Every time the doctor comes, there's another fee to pay. The herbs cost more and more. My brother said the doctor in the county town told him an imported drug is available now, highly effective but expensive. Now that I work in the city, my sister-in-law wants to hire someone to look after Ma. Gupin smiled. "This room may look bad to you, but I don't mind. I come from a village a lot poorer than this. Besides, I spend most of my time in the office."

He licked his lips. "Many migrant workers live here, families with children. Little Mountain and his wife are next door. They're from the same area as me. Whenever one of us goes home, the other can send messages or a food parcel. We help each other."

Little Mountain bustled in with a steaming bowl. He said something to Gupin in their dialect, then told Mei, with a smile, as he put the bowl on the window sill to cool, "My wife made chicken soup. When will the doctor come?"

"He should be here soon."

"I'll fetch him from the bridge."

"But you've never met him. How will you know him?"

"He's coming in a taxi. I'll ask." He went out again.

"It was all my fault. So stupid." Gupin leaned back against the pillows and sighed. "I was too close to the cars. The roads were slippery and snow was lashing down. I should have taken the bus instead of my bicycle but I didn't want to be late. I know you have to settle the case of the boy who died in hospital before I go home." He looked at his broken leg. "Now I can't travel anyway. But I haven't seen my mother for a year and we've always been together for the Spring Festival."

"Maybe we can keep each other company. My sister's taking my mother to Canada. Now, eat some soup." Mei plumped the pillows and helped Gupin to sit up. She saw that moving hurt him: sweat had broken out on his forehead. "Do you need a painkiller?"

Gupin shook his head. "It's not too bad."

Mei spooned up some soup, blew gently to cool it, then lifted it to Gupin's mouth. Their eyes met. Then the soup touched Gupin's lips. He swallowed it, and the moment was gone. They both spoke at once: Gupin asked about the case of the dead boy, and Mei about his neighbourhood.

"Oh, all sorts of people live here," he said. "There are two sisters who work in salons ..."

"I haven't done much since you put the files together for me. I've started on a new case, a pop star ..."

They chuckled.

"A pop star!" exclaimed Gupin. "Anyone I might know?"

"Have you heard of a singer called Kaili?"

"The one who sang the theme to *Knights of Heaven*?"

"I'm impressed," said Mei, the corners of her mouth curling up. She fed Gupin more chicken soup while she told him what she'd discovered. Gupin listened, spellbound.

"I was convinced, especially after I'd seen all the drink, pills and cigarettes in her apartment, that Kaili was a diva who lived on the edge. But the letters from L changed my mind. There is more to her than meets the eye. I want to find out more about L. Maybe he was an artist. I wish you could see the paper butterfly. It's a work of art. I'd never seen anything like it." Mei sighed. "But I think she's forgotten him. She hadn't touched those letters for a long time."

"Do you think L has something to do with Kaili's disappearance?"

"No. But he might be the person to tell me about the real Kaili. I hope that will help me find her."

"I wish I could help," said Gupin, when the soup was gone.

"You concentrate on getting better. That's what you can do," said Mei.

The door opened and Little Mountain ushered in the doctor. Ding was a year younger than Mei, stout with a round, kind face. He believed he had been wrong to study medicine. His first love, as he had discovered when the computer arrived in China, was electronics. Now he spent his spare time mending computers, radios and televisions.

"Thank you for coming." Mei got up to greet her friend.

Ding took off his glasses and, with his fingers, wiped off the steam that had clouded them. He put them back on. "Let me have a look at the patient."

He examined Gupin, asking about the accident and the surgery. Gupin described how he was hit by a car while he was riding his bicycle in the snow and how passers-by had taken him to hospital where they had operated on his broken leg. Little Mountain stood next to them, interrupting from time to time with his version of events.

Ding asked Gupin to unbutton his shirt so that he could listen to his chest.

Mei went outside. There was a frozen rubbish heap by the entrance to the courtyard. Someone had just thrown a few rotten cabbages onto it. The scene reminded Mei of her childhood. She must have been seven or eight years old when something had happened with her mother's work and they had had to move again. She remembered sitting on the doorstep at a courtyard house, not much different from this one, making coal balls with powdered coal and water. The skin on her hands had cracked and bled.

While they made the balls, they discussed their new home. Mama had said they were lucky to be able to heat the room with the stove but told Mei and Lu not to play close to it. Then they talked about Mei's new school in the village. Mei said they had the same kind of stove in their classroom. But she didn't tell Mama about the ash in her desk or how the peasant boys beat her in the playground. She asked Mama when Baba would come home from the labour camp. Mama said, the lips twitching into a smile, that she hoped soon.

But he never did.

As Mei stood in the snow, anger surged through her. For the past twenty years she had loved and comforted her mother in her loss. But then she had discovered her betrayal. She had denounced their father, sending him to his death. She had hidden the truth from her children.

Yet hadn't she loved and protected her daughters? Mei remembered the hardship and their mother's determination to rise above it for her children's sake. She remembered her eyes, kind but sad, and her embrace, always a little too tight. Perhaps she had suffered too, and repented. She had never remarried. She had devoted herself to her dead husband's children. The wind howled, lashing Mei's face and hands. She pulled her hat low and adjusted her scarf, then went back inside.

Ding was packing his instruments. "You must take care. Any more complications and you'll be back in hospital," he told Gupin. Seeing Mei, he added, "I'll need to go to my old hospital and ask a friend to prescribe the medicine."

"Let me drive you."

"Thank you, Doctor," said Gupin. "How much do I owe you?"

"Nothing," Ding waved a hand casually. "You will pay only for the medicine."

Mei smiled at her old friend. When they were children, Ding had taught her how to catch shrimp using alcohol-marinated meat as bait and an old net shopping-bag. It was a game they played every summer by the city moat.

They said goodbye to Gupin. Little Mountain insisted on walking them out of the village. As they navigated through the winding alleys, Mei asked after Ding's parents, both retired doctors.

"Ma's happy. She goes to the Revolutionary Retired Comrades Association three times a week and learns ballroom dancing. Ba is having a tough time of it. He's been talking to his old work unit about helping on certain cases. He thinks they can do with his expertise."

"Will they pay him?"

"Some people get rich doing post-retirement consulting, but my ba doesn't care about money. He's just bored with staying at home. He can't cook, do laundry or shop for groceries. He drives Ma crazy with his short temper."

Mei smiled. "I love your ma. She's so kind. I've never seen her lose her temper."

"Unless my sister is mentioned. She's moved in with her boyfriend and Ma's furious. Ba won't even talk to her."

"You mean the German?"

"Yes."

"Will they get married?"

"You sound just like my ma. We don't know. But it doesn't matter, not these days. I tried to tell my parents that it's the modern way."

"What do they say?"

"Ba won't listen. He's dealt with all kinds of accidents, natural disasters and nationwide outbreaks of disease, but he can't come to terms with his unmarried daughter sharing her home with a man."

"A foreigner too. Maybe your father thinks of them as enemies still?" Mei teased.

"How did you guess?"

"You're joking."

"Ba never jokes."

Soon they reached the wooden bridge and said goodbye to Little Mountain. Further in the distance, behind the smog, the city loomed, with its modern apartment buildings and vast high-rises.

17

Mei dropped Ding at the hospital where he had once worked, made a U-turn and was about to drive away when her mobile phone rang. Mr Peng's distraught voice said, "They've found her."

"Who did?"

"The police called. I've sent Manyu to identify her body."

Mei gasped. "Her body? Where is it?"

"In an abandoned factory in Dashanzi. Manyu has no experience in dealing with the police. Can you go and make sure she doesn't say anything stupid?" Mr Peng asked. "Let me know what you find out." He hung up.

Mei put away her phone, and sped off.

Dashanzi – Big Mountain – was a flat area sandwiched between Bright Horse River and the Airport Expressway. It was once the industrial corner of Beijing, with state-owned factories making electrical components. Many had gone out of business or relocated to the provinces. The work-unit compounds, where thousands of workers and their families had lived, were now empty. The local economy had collapsed. The unemployed – 'waiting-for-work youths', as the Party referred to them – hung around causing trouble. Many taxi drivers refused to go there even in daylight.

In Dashanzi Mei drove down what looked like a busy street. Power lines tangled from one leaning pole to another. Makeshift huts lined the street. A four-storey building stood alone by the roadside. A character "*Chai*" – "to be demolished" – had been painted in white on its walls. Cyclists rode up and down. A few shoppers ambled along.

Mei stopped by a police kiosk but no one was inside. She looked around, saw an old lady staggering out of an alleyway, and asked for directions to the Dashanzi police station.

"Why are you asking?" She leaned on her walking-stick.

Instantly Mei knew that she'd run into one of those old women who wanted to know everything. She tried to sound patient, and smiled, when she said, "I have business there."

"What kind of business?" She ground her few remaining teeth.

"Official."

"If it's official business, why don't you know where the police station is?"

"Old Mama, do you or don't you know where the station is?"

"Of course I do. I've lived here all my life. It's over there." She lifted her left arm.

Mei thought she was pointing. "Down that street? How far?"

"Over there!" the old lady said impatiently, and waddled away.

Mei found no police station where the woman had indicated. She drove around for a bit, then got out again. The wind was bitterly cold. She looked up and down the street, but there was only grey gloom. A group of youths walked by, slouching through the snow. They eyed Mei provocatively. She turned to look the other way. After another ten minutes, she stopped a father and son. The father told her that the police station had moved eight years ago. He stood on the kerb and gestured at the road crossing. "Go down there, turn right, pass a small bridge, and you will see it."

But Mei didn't find it until she drove to the end of the street where a signpost marked "Police Station" stood beside a frozen puddle. She parked her car and walked down a snowy path. She passed two small shops, then stopped in front of the police station. A sign on the left-hand door read "Hukou Registration" and another on the right, "Public Inquiry". To avoid the long queue for the latter, she went to the residence permit – hukou – registration room. Three policewomen were sorting booklets. Mei told them why she'd come and asked where to go.

"Inside the station, through the side door," they told her.

Mei walked round the building, where she came to a sudden standstill, awed by the sight that confronted her. A grand arch led into an open courtyard so large that no fewer than three inner courtyards led off it. A hundred years ago, Mei guessed, the house would have belonged to a wealthy landlord or even a minor court official. Under the arch hung two red banners. One read "Serving the People" and the other "It's Glorious to be the People's Police". Below them were photographs of all the policemen at the station, in rank order. All twenty faces wore wide grins.

A policeman came out of the inner court swinging a pair of handcuffs. He stopped Mei as she walked through the arch. "Who are you looking for?" He was wearing a long padded coat but no hat.

"Ms Manyu from Guanghua Record Company. She's here to identify a body."

The policeman shifted his weight on to one leg. He looked at Mei suspiciously. "What body?"

Mei wondered if Mr Peng had given her the correct police station. "A famous singer's," she ventured.

The policeman rocked. He tossed the handcuffs from one hand to the other. Another officer came out. "Is there anyone here from a record company?" the first asked him. He kept his eye on Mei.

"She's in the visitor's room with the Twins."

The first policeman spat. "You can go inside," he told Mei.

She crossed the courtyard, went along a narrow path and into the second courtyard. The station reminded her of the Ministry of Public Security. When she had accompanied her boss on field trips, they had gone to district police stations, but never to a local one like this. Wherever they had gone, they had been ushered around by the police chief and his senior officers, then served tea in the best room.

How things had changed, Mei thought. She was a civilian now, so even the lowest-ranking policeman could treat her as if he were a tiger.

The visitors' room was in the inner courtyard. It had an old-fashioned latticed door, the openings glazed with thin rice paper. Mei knocked lightly on its delicate frame.

A male voice told her to come in.

She opened the door and saw Manyu sitting on a sofa, huddling over a teacup as if it were a vital source of warmth. Two uniformed officers were in the room, but sitting at a table in the corner. One was poking about in his mouth with a toothpick. The other had been speaking to Manyu, but when Mei walked in he broke off and came over to her. "You must be Miss Wang. Miss Manyu told us you would be coming. I'm Officer Li." He extended his hand.

Mei shook it. The other policeman put the toothpick into his pocket and stood up. Mei shook hands with him too. He said his name was Gao.

When they stood side by side, they looked like twin brothers. Both were in their twenties, short, with round, glowing faces. Mei guessed that they had not long been out of the police academy.

"We've just come back from identifying the body. I'm afraid Miss Manyu is a little shaken," said one.

Mei turned. Manyu's face was vacant and her eyes hovered on the coffee-table.

"She'll have recovered soon," said Li.

"We've seen it before. It's upsetting for ordinary people to see a body," Gao added. "There's nothing we can do. They have to get over it in their own time."

Li gestured Mei to a seat at the table. "Our instructors warned us of something like this when we were at the academy," he said. "Trauma hits people in different ways."

"She was fine when she saw the body," said Gao, as if to reassure Mei.

"Where is it? Can I see it?" Mei asked.

"At the hospital."

"We have to check with our senior officers."

"Do you know the cause of death yet?"

"No. But we think someone killed her. There was a lot of blood, wasn't there?" They looked at each other and nodded.

"Were you the first on the scene?"

"Yes. We're neighbourhood police. Whenever something happens in our area, we go to find out about it."

"But now Homicide's taken over the case."

"So it is a murder?" said Mei.

"Of course. You don't find someone like her in that kind of place. As soon as I saw her face, I knew I'd seen her somewhere. Didn't I say so, Gao? I thought and thought, and then I remembered. People say TV's bad for you and magazines are rubbish. But how else would you learn about our new society? Am I right, Gao? Well, we identified the victim straight away." Clearly Li was proud of their achievement. He leaned back in his chair and stretched out his legs.

"I wonder how she got there," Mei thought aloud.

"Kidnapping." Gao nodded with conviction. "These days nobody's safe. All sorts of gangs are coming in from the provinces. They are bandits, *tufei*. You'd think they'd been eradicated, killed off by the Communist Party in the civil war fifty years ago, but they're back. Have you heard about the Dongbei *tufei*? They can kill without blinking an eye. Then there are the South of Yangtze River *tufei*. They're cunning. A young woman like Kaili gets into a taxi. The driver sets off — and *bang*! She's kidnapped and locked up in a *tufei* safe-house. If her family doesn't pay up, she's dead."

Mr Peng hadn't mentioned a ransom, thought Mei.

Li waved a hand, stopping his partner. "Enough." He looked at Mei. "Homicide said they'd like to talk to you."

Mei wondered what Manyu had told them.

"Detective Zhao thinks you may have information that will help find the killer." Li threw a thinly disguised smirk at Gao. Mei had a feeling they didn't like Detective Zhao.

"We'll let him know you've arrived." They stood up and left.

Mei sat down beside Manyu, who began to talk, unprompted. "Mr Peng sent for me. He said the police had called. They had found a body in Dashanzi. They thought it was Kaili. He asked me to identify it."

"How did it go?"

Manyu looked at her. Tears were welling in her eyes. "It's not fair. She was so beautiful. But in that place, her hair was stuck together in clumps with blood and her face — disgusting — was frozen in a grey colour. Oh, it was horrible." Manyu shuddered. "I thought about how she must have struggled through the last few minutes of her life. I didn't want to, but I couldn't help thinking how she must have suffered. And to think I hated her — but for what? Petty things that don't really matter. She had her moods, but I was jealous — I resented everything she had. Her looks, her money, her fame, the way men threw themselves at her ...

"I'm sorry I lied to you. I wasn't outside her dressing room that night. I went to see friends. I didn't care what she might want. My parents taught me to be kind and I've failed them. I said nasty things about Kaili. I leaked stories about her to the press. At times I even wished something terrible would happen to her." Tears rolled down her cheeks. "Now that she's dead, I can do nothing to make up for that."

Mei took a packet of tissues out of her handbag and gave it to Manyu. She didn't think she could offer the kind of comfort Manyu needed. Instead she thought of L, the letters she had found in Kaili's apartment and the paper butterfly. A sense of loss flooded her.

Ten minutes later, Detective Zhao came in, a scruffy man in his early thirties, tall and thin. He hardly had time to introduce himself before he was coughing furiously. Eventually he took out a blue checked handkerchief and wiped his mouth.

"Whatever the Twins told you isn't true," he said, pulling up a chair and sitting down across from the sofa. "At one time a brain was considered essential at the police academy, but these days, no one wants to be a low-paid policeman."

He fixed his eyes on Mei. "I've already spoken with Comrade Manyu, who has been very co-operative. I understand Mr Peng hired you to look for Kaili. Why?"

"Business reasons."

"Are you sure?"

"Why don't you ask Mr Peng?"

"I shall," countered Detective Zhao.

"Is this an official interview?"

"We're just chatting, aren't we?"

"But there's been a murder."

"Who said so?"

He went into another bout of coughing. Mei and Manyu looked at each other. Behind them, daylight penetrated the rice paper on the door, casting formless shadows.

"I see that the Twins have been telling you things," said Detective Zhao, when he had stopped coughing. "They're very proud that they recognised Kaili, think themselves very clever. But they're community policemen who never go out of their duty areas. They believe whatever the Street and Hutong Revolutionary Committee tells them ..." He paused. "Comrade Wang Mei," he went on, "we've met before, but I suppose you don't remember. It was in 1990, on the first anniversary of June the fourth. There was a ceremony at the Ministry of Public Security to celebrate exceptional police performance at that time. I was one of those honoured. I was introduced to you. We shook hands."

Mei remembered the occasion, but vaguely. After all, it had been a long time ago. In the years she had worked at the ministry, there had been many such events, all tediously similar.

Detective Zhao went on, "I remember sitting in the audience and wondering who the handsome young woman sitting with the big bosses was. Afterwards we talked about you – we were impressed by your success."

"Oh." Mei gave a short, almost embarrassed laugh, but she was flattered. She was reminded of the good times and the great future she had once believed hers. But it had been an illusion, she told herself, eventually replaced by reality.

And Detective Zhao had once been a star then, she thought, so why is he working now at a small station in Dashanzi? Mei studied him. His uniform was clean but crumpled. It had been washed too many times. His boots were worn. He was pale – and there was that cough. She suspected that his promise, like hers, had been unfulfilled.

"How strange that we should meet again like this. I understand you're no longer with the ministry and are running your own private business. Have you become rich?"

"I manage."

"More than that! The red Mitsubishi outside is yours, isn't it?"

Mei wondered what else he had found out about her.

"When did Mr Peng hire you?"

"Yesterday."

Detective Zhao sniggered. "So you haven't had much of a head start."

"Not at all." Mei waited. She expected Detective Zhao would soon point out that private investigation was illegal in Beijing. If he did, thought Mei, she would have to deny it. Like many private detectives, she had registered her company as an information consultancy to get around the official restriction.

But he didn't.

"Can I see the body?" she asked.

"Too late." The detective consulted his watch. "But I'll arrange for you to view it tomorrow. After all, we aren't strangers to each other." He stood up and smiled with the confidence of a chess player who had just made a clever move.

18

Mei lived in a *jumin xiaochun* — a residential development. Fourteen years ago her landlord had been given the one-bedroom apartment in which she lived by his work unit, but he had never occupied it. He, his wife and their two sons lived in West City District, in a two-bedroom apartment given to his wife by her work unit. Mei's apartment had stood empty for many years and one of Beijing's ring roads was built in front of it. When property ownership had been thrown open to all, her landlord had bought the place for a nominal amount, put in a vinyl floor and let it. As a tenant, Mei was isolated from her neighbours, who had worked together for years. That didn't bother her: she liked her privacy. Of course, her neighbours took every opportunity to peep through her door or eavesdrop on her conversations. Some, like old Mrs Yang, stopped her on the stairs when they met and wanted to know everything that was going on in her life.

Mei parked her car at the side of her building, half on the path. A single street lamp glowed. As usual, the entrance was blocked by bicycles. Mei moved two out of her way and went up the stairs. No one had painted the walls for fourteen years. They had turned grey and were spattered with graffiti. Mei climbed slowly. She was tired. As she set off up the last flight the timer turned off the light and she continued in the dark. She reached the top, dropped her bag on the floor, switched on the light again and unlocked her door.

The apartment was stiflingly hot. The central heating, controlled by the boiler for the entire development, was at full throttle. None of the radiators had thermostats, so Mei couldn't regulate the temperature. She shut the door, went to the living room and opened the window.

Then she threw herself on to the sofa and called Mr Peng on his mobile. "It's Mei. I've come back from Dashanzi police station."

But Mr Peng interrupted her. "Let's not talk on the phone. Can you come to see me?"

Mei was annoyed. She had only just got home. "Is that really necessary?"

"Yes. I'm having dinner at my club. Come and join me. The food here is good."

"I've had dinner," Mei said, "but I'll come. Where's your club?"

Lights blazed at the Hot Bed Club, illuminating the whole compound, as Mei pulled into the car park. A young man ran over to her and directed her to a space. The Hot Bed Club had been opened a year ago by a famous actor who had made his name playing Communist heroes in anti-Japanese, Second World War epics. It occupied twenty acres in Haidian District, and was built in the style of the old peasant houses, each of which had been equipped with a *kang*, or hot bed, typical of the northern Chinese countryside. They were made of mud with a stove underneath to keep the bed warm in the winter.

The club included many high-ranking officials, and senior military figures who had fought the Japanese, among its membership. It reminded them, apparently, of the 'good old days'.

Because it was enclosed by a high wall, everyone was curious about what went on inside it. Rumour ran rife, but no one knew for certain whether the officials actually slept with the tea girls, or if it was here that the deputy mayor had struck his corrupt deals before he was caught out. Equally no one knew whether the corruption charge was based on actual crime or if the case had been brought to exact political revenge.

A young girl led Mei to Mr Peng. She wore a padded *dajin* with silk-knot buttons and carried a red lantern with the word 'luck' – *fu* – on it. They walked across the snowy courtyard to a building adorned by two large red lanterns. A reversed *fu* poster, which signified the coming of luck, hung outside. The girl, who hadn't spoken, opened the door and bowed. Mei went in. The door closed.

The hot bed occupied the entire back wall. Mr Peng sat on it with his legs crossed, the top buttons of his shirt undone.

Plates of hot food, a rice wine ewer and two cups stood on a low table in front of him. A tea girl dressed in peasant costume was kneeling in front of the bed, checking the stove. Another busied herself at a small stove in the corner, warming food, rice wine and hot towels.

Across the table from Mr Peng, Miss Pink was reclining on a stack of silk quilts and embroidered pillows. She wore a low-cut pink dress and her hair was tied into a bun at the back of her head, a few loose strands hanging down her neck. Her cheeks were flushed with alcohol.

"There you are! Come and sit on the bed," called Mr Peng. His eyes were bloodshot.

Mei looked for a chair.

Miss Pink stood up and went to sit beside Mr Peng. "Take our guest's coat," she ordered the tea girl tending the fire under the bed.

"Come here. It's warm on the bed," Mr Peng urged.

Reluctantly Mei sat on the edge. A tea girl came over to remove her shoes. "No!"

The girl was startled and looked at Mr Peng.

"Don't be shy," he said.

"I don't want anyone to take my shoes," snapped Mei. She had thought Mr Peng would show some sign of grief, and she hadn't expected Miss Pink to be there. She was confused as well as angry.

Mr Peng laughed. "As you please. Tell me, have they established the cause of death?"

"No. But they are treating it as murder."

"With what motive?"

"It's too early to say. Detective Zhao is the officer in charge. He is suspicious that Kaili hadn't been reported missing."

"Did you tell him why I hadn't called the police?"

"I did, but he said he'd like to interview you."

"He would!" Mr Peng put down his chopsticks. "A Dashanzi detective wants to question me. Perhaps he plans to summon me to Dashanzi police station."

Miss Pink giggled and poured him some rice wine.

Mr Peng took a sip and shook his head. "Clearly he has no idea. I don't talk to just anyone! And the local police forces are utterly incompetent. They do more harm than good."

Miss Pink ordered more food and drink from one of the tea girls. Mei had a feeling that Miss Pink was not new to the club.

"I've nothing to hide," Mr Peng added, putting a roasted peanut into his mouth and crunching it. "With Kaili, it was straightforward. I was warned so many times against taking her on. But I didn't listen – I didn't want to listen. She played with fire." Mr Peng cast a glance at Miss Pink. "I suppose I wanted to help her. I had a feeling that she'd end up badly so I gave her money, a car and an apartment. I tried to keep her out of trouble. Sometimes a powerful man comes to think of himself as the Spirit of Protection."

"Don't blame yourself. You were good to her, but she never respected you," Miss Pink reminded him.

"I gave her everything and made her a star. But it wasn't enough. She always wanted more – I don't know what of and I doubt she did either."

Mr Peng gestured for his cup to be refilled. "What is your fee? Send me a bill," he said, without looking at Mei.

"You wish me to end the investigation? But Kaili has died – don't you want to know why?"

"Of course I do. But I have a business to worry about. A missing person is one thing, but murder? We can't be dragged into that. As far as you're concerned, Kaili has been found, may she rest in peace. You will be paid. From now on I shall deal with the matter myself."

"Bring our guest's coat," Miss Pink told a tea girl.

"Kaili is no longer your responsibility," said Mr Peng, with a smile. "By the way, your sister and Li-ning are here tonight. I bumped into them on my way in. Would you like to see her?"

Mei stood up, took her coat and put it on.

"I'll ask one of the girls to take you to her," said Mr Peng. "Goodbye."

A path wound across the white courtyard like a long, elegant calligraphy stroke. The tea girl led the way with a red *fu* lantern past brightly lit houses. Mei wondered what secrets lay behind those windows. Another red lantern was making its way across the other end of the courtyard.

This was a little haven for the rich and powerful who had the means to reinvent reality, thought Mei. But what kind of reality?

As Mei approached an open door, she saw Lu and her husband. They seemed to be entertaining businessmen. Her beautiful sister sat at the top of the *kang* surrounded by men in suits. They were laughing, and she heard Li-ning's voice. A few tea girls, half reclining on the *kang*, drank rice wine with them. Others hurried around with replenishments.

Mei stopped short of going inside. "Please take me back to the entrance," she told the tea girl. "I'd rather go home."

She emerged from the Hot Bed Club and stood on the threshold of the sprawling city. She thought of Kaili and L, injustice and guilt. She knew she must continue with the case. She owed it to Kaili, L and those students who had gone into the streets during that fateful spring nine years ago. She owed it to herself too. She had failed to join them then, so she would not desert them now, for justice.

19

In the early morning Mei drove back to Dashanzi. The sunlight was shining on the snow, dazzling her, and the sky was blue with threads of thin cloud.

Detective Zhao's office was a small corner room in the second inner courtyard, warmed by a coal stove. He greeted Mei with a handshake and asked her to sit down. "Tea or boiled water?" he asked, putting another cup on his desk.

"Do you have Oolong tea?"

"I'm afraid not."

"Boiled water, then, please."

Detective Zhao poured some from a green Thermos and handed the cup to Mei. "I've been thinking. You're a college graduate and were at the ministry. You must be clever. There isn't anyone like you here. Actually, there's no one here at all — I'm the homicide department and only on paper at that. Dashanzi isn't a violent area. There's plenty of crime, but mostly petty offences, like robbery or street fighting. We also have many migrant workers."

Detective Zhao coughed, even more violently than he had yesterday. He had to blow his nose frequently too.

"But there's a difficulty." He rubbed his hands.

"Which is?"

"You work for Mr Peng."

Mei took a sip of water. "Not any more. I was dismissed last night. Mr Peng made me go all the way to Haidian District so he could tell me in person."

"Then why are you here?"

"I have my reasons. Also, I thought I'd let you know that Mr Peng doesn't want a murder associated with his company. He'll try to have it covered up."

Detective Zhao coughed for almost a minute. "In that case, we'd better get going." He put on his police cap and padded green coat, then opened the door. Winter sunshine poured into the room. Mei followed him outside.

They walked across the courtyard and turned into a passage that led to the outer courtyard. At the corner, Detective Zhao stopped and pushed open a door.

Inside, the Twins were playing cards.

"What are you doing here?" he demanded. "I asked you to go and talk to the Street and Hutong Committee."

"You didn't say when," said one.

"It's early yet," said the other.

Mei couldn't tell which was Li and which was Gao. The more she studied them, the more alike they seemed.

"You'll need every minute you've got. As I told you, you must question everyone, not just the committee chairwoman."

"What kind of information do you want?"

"Who lives there, how many, whether they've seen or heard anything suspicious in the past few days – I don't know! Use your heads."

"Should I ask about blackmail? I bet that's at the root of it," said the man Mei believed was Li.

"No. Robbery's more likely," Gao disagreed.

Detective Zhao ground his teeth.

"All right! We're going!"

Slowly the Twins put on their coats and left.

"And don't stop on the way for fried breadsticks and hot soya milk," Detective Zhao called after them.

He grunted as he watched them leave. "They don't like to take orders from me. They're second cousins of the director for Housing Control, and one day they'll have my job! Yes! It's the Improving Police Force Education Level Initiative. Eventually every officer will have a college certificate. Unfortunately I never graduated. I had one more year to go at the academy when June the fourth happened. The situation was so bad that we were taken out and put on the streets to work alongside the People's Liberation Army. Then martial law was declared."

At the end of a path, they came to a few rickety huts. A piece of new timber, probably stolen, stuck out from a roof at a dangerous angle, and power lines stretched haphazardly between the dwellings.

"This area used to be full of those huts. Then the district and town government decided to redevelop it, but those people refused to leave. They said they didn't want to go further out of the city, but really they wanted more money. They've miscalculated. One day the government will send down a bulldozer and they'll be homeless."

They passed the huts and turned on to a wider street of small shops. Detective Zhao was striding along. "I hope you don't mind," he said to Mei, steam puffing from his mouth, "but we'll walk to the hospital."

They went in through a door with a red cross painted on it. Inside, the lobby was lit by a few bare bulbs. There was a long queue in front of the pharmacy window.

Detective Zhao took the stairs and Mei hurried to keep up. They went to the first floor. The corridor was filled with people. Patients sat on benches or leaned against the wall, waiting for their names to be called, family and friends crowding around them. As soon as a door opened, a mob tried to surge through. Some demanded to know when their turn would be. Others complained that so-and-so had been allowed in before them.

Detective Zhao shoved his way through the crowd. He moved with enough confidence to make people stop and look at him. When they saw his uniform, they quietened and tried to move out of his way.

At the end of the corridor they came to a set of doors with "Restricted Area" painted on it. They went through, and the noise from the corridors died away. Detective Zhao stopped at another door with a sign that read "Laboratory". He knocked and entered without waiting for an answer.

"You're here!" croaked a voice from behind a stack of tubes.

A man in a white coat emerged. He was small with short hair and little round eyes. His brows were thick and linked above his nose. He looked about ten years older than Detective Zhao.

"Lao Li, Comrade Wang Mei." Detective Zhao made the introduction casually. It seemed the two men knew each other.

Lao Li dried his hands on a towel and extended one to Mei. "Good morning," he said. He turned to Detective Zhao with a smile. "I saw your wife, my Second Sister, at the market yesterday. She told me the good news. Two new apartments!"

Detective Zhao peeled off his coat. "Two or one, no one's sure yet. You know how these things work. It's Beijing Second Radio Manufacturer's housing. They've agreed to give our station two units. But someone's son or nephew may still pop out of nowhere and take one from us."

"Will you get one this time? You've waited years."

"I don't know. I've enough points as far as age and tenure go, but they're always changing the scoring system."

"Second Sister has always wanted one of those modern apartments. She said the construction is almost finished, in the new development area. Have you seen it?"

"She's made me go there many times." Detective Zhao smiled bitterly and blew his nose. "Comrade Wang Mei is here to see the body," he added.

"I'll take you in a minute," said Lao Li, "but first let me give you this." He went to a desk in the corner and came back with a clear plastic bag. "These belonged to the dead girl." He held it up. Inside were two earringclips. "They were found by the body."

Detective Zhao stuffed the bag into his pocket.

Lao Li led them into the next room. The curtains were drawn, and it was very cold, smelling of bleach. In the shadows, Mei made out a stack of medicine boxes. Two industrial refrigerators hummed.

Lao Li opened the curtains. A hospital bed on wheels stood by the window. A body lay on it, covered with a white sheet.

"Have you seen corpses before?" asked Lao Li.

Mei nodded.

"Then remember that whatever they were in life – man, woman, beautiful, ugly, rich, poor, good, evil – everyone's the same when they die, an empty shell."

Lao Li pulled back the sheet halfway.

Kaili's face was bluish white. A cut across her cheek had distorted her features, making her nose crooked. Her lips were pale purple. Her hair looked as if it had been glued to her skull. Her beauty had gone. In fact, it was hard to imagine that there had been life within that shell.

"The cause of death?" enquired Detective Zhao.

Lao Li lifted Kaili's head, turned it and parted her hair to reveal a deep cut.

"The weapon?" asked Detective Zhao.

"Something narrow but blunt."

"Like a metal bar?"

"Possibly. From what I can tell, she's been dead for three days."

Detective Zhao nodded. "That means she died on the day of the snow."

Mei stared at the body. She couldn't decide which was more real to her: the singer in the video, alive and beautiful, whom she had never met, or the body.

Half an hour later, Mei was back on the main street. Fluffy white clouds sailed in the sky.

"Are you ready for lunch?" asked Detective Zhao.

Mei shook her head. She couldn't think of eating so soon after their session with Lao Li.

"I'm famished. I've been up since dawn," said Detective Zhao. "And as it usually takes the Twins a long time to gather information, we'll go to a place I know."

The restaurant was called the East Wind Pavilion. It was attached to a small hotel. As soon as they entered, a fat man with a double chin hurried over to them, smiling.

"Welcome, comrades!" He shook hands with Detective Zhao, one eye on Mei. "A beautiful day! Will it remain like this for the Spring Festival?"

"Mr Liang is the manager here," Detective Zhao told Mei, but he didn't introduce them.

Nonetheless Mr Liang shook hands with her. "Just two for lunch?" he asked.

"Yes," Detective Zhao said, and walked towards the back.

"The inner room, please," Mr Liang said quickly, running after the detective. "I heard about the big case." He had lowered his voice.

Detective Zhao frowned. "Which one?"

"The murder, of course," he said dramatically. "Comrade Li and Comrade Gao called earlier for fried breadsticks and hot soya milk. The murder of a pop star! I was horrified." He squeezed his eyes shut. "Ah, you have a cold too! My brother-in-law has been ill for weeks. This miserable winter, five storms so far. Soon we'll all be ill." Mr Liang took two quick steps and opened the door to a private dining room, small and windowless. The light-coloured carpet showed a few large stains. A big round table and ten high-backed chairs took up almost all the space.

Detective Zhao sat down and blew his nose again.

Mr Liang smiled, his double chin stretching into one. "You're in luck, Comrade Zhao. We have some juicy pig's trotters."

"You like them?" Detective Zhao asked Mei. He searched his pockets for cigarettes.

"Trotters!" Mei exclaimed. "I thought no one ate them any more. When we were growing up, they were my mother's favourite."

Mr Liang beamed. "In the Cultural Revolution pig's trotters were a delicacy. Meat was hard to find. Today everywhere you turn there's another Guangdong seafood restaurant. People compete to spend the most on one fish, sometimes thousands of yuan because it was imported from Australia. We do honest meals here. You won't find trotters anywhere else."

Detective Zhao found his cigarettes in his trouser pocket. "You have trotters because everyone around here is a peasant." He stuffed a cigarette into his mouth. Mr Liang lit it for him.

Detective Zhao turned to Mei. "This is a restaurant we like. No nonsense, no gimmicks. When I'm on night duty, I bring my men here for a snack. The owner is an old factory hand. We know him well."

At once Mei knew what kind of restaurant this was — a place where the police could eat for nothing. In return, they would warn the owner in advance of inspections.

"Mr Liang, what else did the Twins talk about?" Detective Zhao asked.

"They told me that your station had 'persuaded' Beijing Second Radio Manufacturer to hand over two apartments from their new housing development. There's going to be a new scoring system to decide who gets them. It'll be achievement-based, they said."

"About the case."

"Only that it was a robbery. They said Dashanzi had never had such a big case before. The district will send someone down to investigate."

Detective Zhao puffed hard. "We're busy, Mr Liang. Can you make sure the food comes quickly?"

"I'll get them started in the kitchen straight away." He bowed and left.

Detective Zhao drew on his cigarette, then let the smoke out. It rose to the ceiling and dissolved.

"The Twins can't wait for someone to come from the district station. They don't care about solving the case. In any event they wouldn't know how to go about it. They just want to impress a higher-ranking official and be promoted." He spat. "The Twins are no good at real work – even if they aren't entirely stupid. But I'm not going to let some district man take over the case from me. I've worked too hard and waited too long."

For what, he didn't say. Mei wondered whether he meant the new apartment, promotion, or both. Her phone rang. It was Manyu. "I'm calling from a public kiosk. Can we meet? I've something to tell you."

"Would you like me to pick you up after work?"

"No. I'd prefer to meet you somewhere."

Mei thought for a second. "We could go to Soya Bean Flower, the Sichuan restaurant chain. There's a branch not far from where you live in Xidan. I passed it yesterday."

"I know it. I've been there with my parents. Six thirty?"

"Yes."

They hung up.

"You *are* rich!" Detective Zhao said, mocking. "A car *and* a mobile phone. Do you own an apartment too? Private work must pay well. I only hope you aren't doing private detective jobs. You wouldn't, would you, knowing that it's illegal?"

Mei narrowed her eyes. "Of course not."

Detective Zhao smiled. He wanted her to know that he knew, but he wasn't going to do anything to harm her as long as they were friendly with each other.

He stubbed out his cigarette in the ashtray. "My wife tells me I shouldn't smoke, but I can't resist it. They shout to me from my pockets, tempting me each time I sit down or when I'm bored. Perhaps you do things you know are bad for you but you can't help it."

He eyed her meaningfully.

Mei wondered what he meant. What wasn't good for her? Running an illegal business or getting involved in Kaili's case? "Don't we all?" She tried to sound light-hearted.

But Detective Zhao wanted to make a point. "Your company is called Lotus Information Consultancy. I like to do my homework. The business is clearly on a good footing. It's made you rich. But I don't envy you. Sometimes it hurts to see friends or colleagues buying cars or going to expensive restaurants — my wife is always nagging me to make money like so-and-so, or go for promotion. Unluckily for her, I don't care about money. I have no more sympathy for the rich than I do for the poor."

Mei realised he was telling her obliquely that he was an honest policeman and she could trust him. "Kaili was rich and famous and you could do well by solving her case," said Mei.

"I'm working on it because it's the right thing to do — and I must get to the bottom of what happened so that my wife will get her new apartment." He lit another cigarette. "But we must move cautiously. There're too many Buddhas to whom we have to *kowtow*. It'll get messy if we're not careful."

"We?"

"You want to solve it as much as I do, although I don't understand why. You certainly won't make money."

"I like a challenge," said Mei.

Detective Zhao stared at her. But Mei didn't want to explain how close she felt now to Kaili. Tiananmen Square had played a part in both their lives, in love lost, hope shattered and faith betrayed.

"You will tell me what you know about her, won't you? Unless we work together, we won't get far," said Detective Zhao.

The door opened and Mr Liang marched in with a parade of four waitresses who carried slow-boiled pig's trotters, cold meat, stir-fried vegetables, rice wine and tea.

20

That afternoon, Detective Zhao and Mei hurried to Factory 958. On the way, Detective Zhao reprimanded a man who was selling firecrackers on the pavement for having no licence to trade. "Don't let me see you when I come back," he warned.

The vendor knew he was in luck. Normally he would have been taken to the police station, fined and his goods confiscated. "I'll sell these last few. I'll soon be off, sir."

At the end of the street they turned east. A snow-covered path ran alongside open fields. A few people were going the same way, pushing bicycles. A donkey cart had made long wheelmarks in the snow. In the fields, black crows pecked hopefully, searching for food.

As they trudged along Detective Zhao talked about the area's history. "The factory made radios like the Red In The East models – do you remember them? They had wooden cases, were heavy and broke regularly. You couldn't get many stations on them. These days, everyone has Japanese radios, so small you can keep them in a pocket. After 'Reform and Open Door', Factory 958 switched to making components for these outdated models, but that business dried up too. At one point there was talk of modernisation, forming a joint-venture with a foreign partner, but it was too late. Guangdong and Zhejiang provinces had many such businesses making radio components.

"Eventually the factory closed. The land and buildings were owned by the government, so both the city and the district claimed them. While they were arguing, the nephew of the director of District Housing Control started letting rooms to migrant workers. He said he had his uncle's permission to do so. Then someone else turned up with permission from the Beijing Housing Reform Bureau to do the same thing. His permit was more influential than the nephew's, but his superiors were further away. The director of District Housing Control is a second cousin of our chief, but as police, we can't be seen to ignore orders from the top. It was a mess. Now, with the murder, everyone will hear of what has been going on at 958."

They passed clusters of bare trees and rows of warehouses, then four or five smaller buildings. Detective Zhao pointed at them. "They used to be workshops but are now empty. The body was found in one."

They passed an old bicycle hut, part of whose roof had caved in, and stopped in front of a three-storey building with large but mostly broken windows. Attached to the front, like giant claws reaching for the sky, were four square ventilation pipes.

Mei made out two faded red revolutionary slogans on the

walls: "Extra Hours With Extra Care For the Sake of Revolution" and "Work Hard and Produce Above Quota".

To the left of the entrance, a flight of stairs led to the upper floors. On the landing a policeman, arms folded, hands stuffed into his sleeves, paced back and forth.

"Where are the Twins?" Detective Zhao called, his voice echoing.

The young policeman took his hands out of his sleeves and straightened his back. "I don't know, sir. I haven't seen them."

Detective Zhao rolled his eyes. "This is Comrade Wang," he said. "We'll take a look at the crime scene."

"Yes, sir." He stood to attention.

Detective Zhao started up the stairs, Mei following. On the landing they saw bloodstains on the stairs and the wall.

"This is where the body was," he said.

Mei inspected the blood. "Can we go further up?"

Detective Zhao nodded. The window above the staircase was broken. Snow had blown in and frozen on the half-landing. They climbed more stairs to the top floor. The corridor was wide but dark. Some doors were missing, through which Mei saw desolate rooms with broken windows, graffiti and drifts of snow.

"People stole the doors to sell or use themselves," said Detective Zhao. "The building is uninhabitable. There's no electricity or water. Even children don't like it here, but some kids came in to play when the snow fell. They found the body."

Mei walked into one of the rooms. It had a high ceiling. From the windows, she could see ramshackle cabins. Thin smoke seeped out of one or two windows.

"Is that where the migrant workers live?" She pointed.

"Yes, in the old factory cabins. Each has been partitioned into small units. Sometimes a family one, sometimes four or five workers together."

"Have you talked to them?" asked Mei.

"I've tried, but every time I approached someone – a woman doing her washing at the public tap, for instance – they ran inside. I questioned some of the men, but whatever I asked, they said they hadn't seen anything. Naturally they're afraid of the police. They don't have legal residence in Beijing so the children can't go to school and run wild on the streets in gangs. Sometimes they steal. Now there's a dead body. Of course everyone's frightened."

"Do you think they had something to do with the murder? What would be the motive?"

"The Twins think a robbery went wrong. I'd love to disagree but I can't come up with anything else. It certainly looks like robbery. Manyu said on the night of the performance that Kaili was wearing two big rings, a watch and a pair of earrings. But we've only found these." From his pocket, he took out the plastic bag Lao Li had given him.

"May I see them?"

Detective Zhao gave her the bag.

She went to the window, opened the bag, took out one of the clips with her fingertips and held it close to her eyes. "But why would they kill her?"

"Maybe they were angry when they discovered the jewels were glass. Maybe she fought them."

"I don't think she was the kind of person to fight for a watch or a pair of earrings. She had plenty more. By the way, the earrings were real – they have the Cartier hallmark."

"What's Cartier?"

"A famous French jeweller, very expensive."

"So it was robbery."

"No."

"But you just said she wore expensive earrings."

"She did. But someone took them only after she'd died. If it had been a robbery, she would have taken them off herself. You wouldn't have found the clips."

Detective Zhao blew his nose. They were silent for a while.

Then voices floated up to them from downstairs. Mei handed the bag back to Detective Zhao and they made their way to the stairs. The Twins were on their way up.

"Where were you?" Detective Zhao barked.

"We wanted to be thorough," said one.

"What did you find out?"

"Migrant workers' children found the body. They roam the factory grounds all day, making trouble," said the other, panting.

"Did you learn anything new?"

"Two mothers saw the body. They told one of the fathers, who reported it to the Street and Hutong Revolutionary Committee."

"And we found out why the man was at home rather than at work. He was sick."

"No, he wasn't. He was doing the night shift."

"Did you talk to mother, father or child?" asked Detective Zhao

"No."

"Who did you talk to?"

"The Street and Hutong Revolutionary Committee, of course."

"But they have nothing to do with the migrant workers."

"They keep an eye on them. They know what's going on."

"Do they?" Detective Zhao said, with irony.

"The migrant workers won't talk to the committee. They're hiding something," said a Twin.

"Or someone," added the other.

"They're probably afraid they'll incriminate themselves." Detective Zhao waved a hand impatiently. "What else did the committee tell you? Have there been any gang activities?"

"There're always people coming and going. Newcomers like to move in with their relatives or old neighbours from their village. No one knows exactly who is here and the situation is getting worse."

They nodded.

"Soon most of them will go home for the Spring Festival and we'll be unable to continue," said Detective Zhao. "Go and find the people who saw the body. Bring them to the station. If they don't want to talk to us here, they will there."

"Do you want them today?"

"Yes." Detective Zhao started down the stairs. The he stopped, and turned: "Don't just stand there! Hurry up!"

"Right." The Twins went down the stairs, dragging their feet at every step.

A new policeman had arrived to guard the crime scene. Detective Zhao spoke to him briefly while Mei continued downwards.

Outside, she put on her hat and gloves. The sun was setting in a pink haze. The air smelled of burning coal.

"I wonder whether she was blackmailed," said Detective Zhao, as they walked towards the street.

"For money?" asked Mei.

"Or something else."

21

It was dark when Mei arrived at Xidan. She parked her car and walked into Xidan North Street. It was packed with holiday shoppers, and snack-sellers shouted their wares – steamed buns, Mongolian lamb kebabs and *nian gou*, sticky rice cakes.

She searched for the Soya Bean Flower restaurant. Under the clear sky, families wandered about happily in the cold, children holding *bingtang hulu*. A teenage girl stared at Mei. She had shining, curious eyes and red cheeks.

When she had been that girl's age, Mei had come shopping in the city centre with her mother. From where they lived, in the far north-west corner of the city, they had had to take a long bus ride, changing twice. As they were prone to motion sickness, they often got off the bus and walked the last three or four miles. Sometimes they'd alight at an unfamiliar stop to explore the neighbourhood and the streets on their way.

The memory of long-gone happiness pricked Mei's heart

like a thorn and made her sad. She remembered how hard it had been for them as outcasts, daughters without a father, a wife without a husband, a mother who was hunted out of every job she had. They had endured so much suffering but the love between them had survived — until the truth about her father's death had come between them. Mei wondered whether such knowledge had hurt her mother, as it hurt her now, for the past twenty-five years. Her poor, sad mother — suddenly she wanted to tell her she still loved her after all. But she couldn't. It was as if a sheet of ice, in the shape of her dead father, stood between them.

Abruptly Mei turned her head. The stars shone pale above the city lights. Then she looked back at the street and saw, through the mist, the yellow and red sign of the Soya Bean Flower restaurant.

Inside, the air reeked of hot chilli, Sichuan peppercorns and herbs. Any lingering thoughts of her mother and their past were forgotten.

The restaurant, crammed with dark tables and high-backed chairs, was full. Customers slurped hot dumplings in red chilli sauce and shovelled mouthfuls of rice after spicy tofu. The noise was deafening. Every now and then, someone shouted to a waitress.

Mei found Manyu sitting at a corner table with her back to the wall. She was playing with her teacup, pushing it around the table, absorbed in her thoughts.

"I'm sorry I'm late. There was heavy traffic on the Airport Expressway," Mei said, as she joined her.

Manyu smiled. "I needed time anyway to think things through."

Mei took off her coat, folded it over the back of the chair and sat down.

"I'm having jasmine tea. Would you prefer something else?"

"Jasmine, please," said Mei. She normally liked Oolong tea, but after a long walk, she was thirsty. Jasmine would be refreshing.

"I'm sorry I can't invite you to my home. The apartment is small and my parents might listen in."

"This is a good place."

"It's very noisy, so no one will overhear us."

Mei nodded. "What was it you wanted to tell me?" She emptied her cup. The tea was stewed and had gone cold.

"I'd like to help," said Manyu, picking up the menu that had been lying on the table, "but should we order first? I'm sure you're hungry."

When they had decided on a few well-known Sichuan dishes, Mei called over the waitress and ordered Husband and Wife Lounge Fillet, Dumplings in Red Water, *ma puo tofu* and Boiled Fish in Forty Spices. "And could we have a fresh pot of tea, please? This one's cold."

"I've been thinking a lot since yesterday," said Manyu. "It was such a shock to me. As you know, I never liked Kaili. She was beautiful and clever, but she took advantage of people. Once she'd got all she could out of them, she dropped them. She was spoilt. She cared little about the feelings of others.

"But did she deserve to die like that? No one does. I couldn't sleep last night. I kept seeing her face, battered and lifeless. What's the use of youth and beauty? Death takes away everything — memories, love, hate, guilt, promise — everything …" She trailed off. After a short silence, she took a sip of tea and went on. "Now that Kaili's dead, I think of her all the time. I remember incidents I thought I'd forgotten and see them differently. I can't tell you how it happened, but it was as if suddenly I understood her. She was unhappy. She didn't know what she wanted. She was restless, always seeking something that wasn't there. Then I thought perhaps she really wanted nothing. She was so sad and hurt that she had no aim in life and no desire to live."

"She didn't kill herself," Mei put in.

"That's not what I meant. Kaili wasn't the kind of person who would commit suicide. She hadn't the courage. But because she didn't value her own feelings, she treated everyone else with contempt."

"But you want to help catch her killer."

"It's strange, I know. I couldn't understand it either. Why would I want to put my job and my future on the line for her? She's dead, and I was never her friend."

Manyu began to push her teacup round again. "I suppose I want to help because she was sad, she had suffered and she had been wronged."

"What do you mean?"

"Did you know that Kaili was Mr Peng's mistress?"

Mei nodded.

"But Mr Peng also took up with his secretary. Many people in the company knew. I don't know why Kaili didn't find out before – perhaps because she never cared for Mr Peng. She was with him for practical reasons.

"The day of the concert at the Capital Gymnasium, Kaili found out about his affair with his secretary. When I saw her, she was extremely short-tempered. I felt sorry for her and tried to comfort her, but she said she didn't want my pity and shouted at me to leave."

"If she didn't love Mr Peng, why would she care?"

"Perhaps he hurt her pride."

Their food came. Two waitresses laid the dishes in front of them and filled their rice bowls. Mei waited till they had gone and asked, "Do you have any idea why she disappeared?"

"I think she was really hurt. She had no friends and now Mr Peng had betrayed her. Perhaps she wanted revenge." Manyu glanced around. When she was sure no one was listening, she whispered, "Rumour runs that Mr Peng got Kaili into drugs."

"Do you think she might have known something about him that he was afraid of?"

Manyu nodded, her eyes shining.

Mei picked up her cup. The usually fragrant jasmine tea tasted of water.

Manyu put a spoonful of *ma pou tofu* on Mei's plate. "I don't know whether any of this is useful, but I thought I'd tell you anyway."

"Thank you," said Mei. The *tofu* burned her tongue, then numbed it.

"If there's anything else I can do to help, let me know," said Manyu.

Mei tore a piece of paper out of her notebook and copied down the dates of Kaili's cash withdrawals. She slid the paper to Manyu. "Can you find out where Kaili might have gone on or around these dates?"

"I'll try. I'll check her diary and with our driver."

"Good." Mei smiled.

The window behind Manyu had fogged. One patch was clearing, water droplets rolling down the glass like tears.

22

The next day Manyu called Mei at lunch time. "I may have found something," she said eagerly. "I checked those dates you gave me in Kaili's diary. On the first, she cancelled two press interviews. On the other two there were no entries at all.

"Then I spoke to our driver. Kaili had used the car on all three days and each time had gone to the Drum Tower. I bought breakfast for the driver. We chatted for a long time. We know each other pretty well …" Manyu paused, "… because we both disliked Kaili. I asked him whether he remembered where she went and for how long. At first he couldn't remember, but then I probed him and he said that each time he'd dropped her off by the Drum Tower in Hind Street and she went into the *hutong*."

"Did he wait for her?"

"Yes, but he can't remember how long she was there for. Our drivers do a lot of runs for different people. They need specific dates and times. They're supposed to record their trips in a log book, but most of them don't bother. Sometimes they jot down the general area they go to. What do you think?"

"Maybe she went to meet someone – in one of the *houhai* restaurants perhaps. Maybe she was being blackmailed, paying someone off," Mei said, as she weighed up the possibilities.

"Any news from the police?" asked Manyu.

"I called Detective Zhao this morning but haven't heard back."

"I hope they find the murderer."

"Thank you for your help," said Mei.

"If there's anything else I can do, please call again."

Then Mei rang Ding. "It's Mei." She spoke rapidly as soon as he answered. "Could you help me again? I'll pay you."

Ding's voice was calm. "What is it?"

"A boy died in hospital after a routine operation. His parents wanted to know what really happened …" She summarised what she had uncovered so far. "Now that Gupin can't work, I wonder if you can step in?"

"I will, if my wife will let me," Ding said. "I suppose she would like the money."

Mei smiled. "Good. I'll drop off the case material. Will you meet me at the gate to your compound? I don't have time to register and go inside. Trying to visit you is like entering a military zone."

"Well, it is an army hospital," said Ding.

Later, after she had seen Ding, Mei drove up the ring road towards South Pound Village. Ding had assured her that Gupin would make a full recovery, but she wanted to check on him and also ask his advice.

She was glad to find him looking better. His face was fresh, and he seemed stronger. The stove burned brightly, filling the room with warmth. Gupin said he was bored with being bed-bound and had been thinking about the dead boy. "So many different versions of the story came from the hospital and the drug companies. It doesn't add up," he said.

"I agree. At the moment I can't see the connection between the two groups, but I'm almost sure there is one. That's why I've asked Dr Ding to help. He was a doctor for many years and now he sells medical equipment. Perhaps some of his contacts can shed light on the case."

Gupin nodded. "He's a good man."

"He said he'd come to see you in a few days."

Mei picked up the kettle from the top of the stove, walked over to the jar by the door and filled it with two calabashes of water.

"How about the other case – Kaili? Are you any closer to finding her?" Gupin asked.

Mei set the kettle back on the stove. "She's been found – at least, her body has."

"She's dead?"

"It looks as if she was murdered."

Mei sat on the stool by Gupin's bed and told him what had happened. Gupin listened, transfixed. Mei took the paper butterfly from her handbag and gave it to him. Lying in the palm of his large hand, it looked vulnerable.

"I found it in Kaili's apartment," said Mei. She told Gupin about L and his letters. "There was a different Kaili inside those letters, idealistic, innocent and reckless. L was thoughtful and cautious. He loved her."

"Do you think he made this paper butterfly?" asked Gupin.

Mei was caught off guard by the question and frowned. "Yes," she said slowly. "Maybe he did. Maybe he was an artist. No. Qingdao University is a science university. It has no art department. But he might have been an amateur artist."

"Or an amateur craftsman," said Gupin, holding up the butterfly and examining it. "At home people make things like this, if not butterflies. Some families had a craft in their ancestry, which was passed down the generations."

"Or he might have bought it from a shop and written his initial on the wing," said Mei, thinking aloud. "He might have made it, but what is it for? Crafts usually have a practical function – at least, originally they did."

"Old people know about crafts. In our village, there's an old man we call Old Grandpa. We think he must be nearly a hundred. He's seen everything and knows everything. We need to find someone like him. But Beijing's too big. It's impossible."

"Not necessarily. L lived in the old *hutong*. Maybe someone there might know about the paper butterfly, if it's a traditional craft."

"There're so many *hutongs* …"

"There was a reference to the Drum Tower in his last letter," Mei said, "and Kaili went to the Drum Tower a few times."

"Do you think it's a coincidence?"

A light seemed to travel across her face. "Maybe not. That's it, Gupin!" Mei exclaimed, grabbing his hands without thinking.

Gupin's face reddened. The paper butterfly fell to the floor. Mei let go.

The kettle boiled, its lid rattling. Steam gushed out of the spout. Mei took it off the heat and closed the stove with an iron plate. She filled Gupin's cup with newly boiled water and handed it to him. "Before I go, I need to ask a favour. Do you know anyone – a migrant worker, I mean – in Dashanzi or, better yet, in Factory 958? Can you find out what they might know about Kaili's death? No one there wants to talk to the police."

"That shouldn't be a problem. I'll ask Little Mountain. He knows a lot of people."

"How will you get the information to me?"

"I'll ask Little Mountain to drop it at the office."

"We'll be in touch." With that, Mei left him. In the courtyard, the thaw had begun.

23

At a quarter past three that afternoon, Mei drove up Drum Tower West Street. It was one of her favourites, especially in summer, when it was shaded by chestnut trees. She parked the car at the roadside next to a large pile of dirty snow.

Away from this street, long, narrow *hutong* stretched out like roots, leading into the labyrinth of Houhai. Mei walked into an alleyway. It was very quiet, and patches of compressed snow glittered under the bright winter sun. A long shadow appeared at the other end and a man came towards her, pushing a bicycle. He stared openly at Mei, as Beijingers do, apparently disapproving.

At the end of the *hutong*, she came to a frozen white lake. Sunshine radiated from its glossy surface. There was a small bar on the corner. Someone had splashed angry words in red paint on its wall: "*Be quiet. I want to sleep. I want to live.*"

Mei walked along the lake, past graceful weeping willows that waited for spring. The ancient neighbourhood was in the midst of renovation. Some houses had been given a coat of grey paint, while others were still shabby and peeling. New bars, built in the traditional style, gleamed, but behind them, old courtyard houses crumbled.

Mei went east, crossing Silver Ingot Bridge. She passed Shao Ro Ji – Roast Meat restaurant. In its car park, well-dressed customers were getting out of their cars.

The road narrowed into a path. The redevelopment had progressed no further. Mei followed the path, which led to the lake, then turned back on itself. She stopped at the curve.

There was a small house. Large patches of paint had peeled off its walls to reveal the plaster. Two fire extinguishers, chained to a metal hook, made a strange display behind a piece of clear plastic under the window. A wooden sign above the door read "Bao Du King".

Mei pulled open the door, parted a quilted curtain and went into the one-room restaurant. It was crammed with dark wooden furniture, some of it stripped of paint. A thick smell of boiled intestines and spicy sauce filled the air. Two elderly men hunched over a table, slurping from bowls. A silver-haired old man, wearing an apron, sat and chatted with them. He was tiny, with a flat, freckled face that was scored with lines as deep as knife cuts. His eyes twinkled as he spoke. It was Bao Du King.

He turned. "*Bao du?*" he asked Mei.

"Yes," Mei said, taking off her coat and sitting at a table.

"How many bowls?"

"One."

"Would you like dry-baked buns too?"

Mei wasn't sure.

"Have you had *bao du* before?"

"No."

"Then have some dry-baked buns," declared Bao Du King. The two elderly men nodded.

"Very well." Mei gave a hesitant smile.

"Tea?"

"Oolong."

"Steal Monk or White Monkey?"

"Steal Monk."

Bao Du King stood up, told the other customers to eat slowly and went into the kitchen.

Mei had read about Bao Du King in the newspapers. He had learned how to quick-fry tripe as a young man in the Muslim district. He had owned a small restaurant in the area until the 1950s when the Smash Four Olds Movement had rooted out traditional Beijing eating-houses. Forty years later, the city government had decided to bring back tradition and redevelop Houhai, so Bao Du King returned to his old business. But the officials were not pleased: they thought *bao du* a dish unworthy of resurrection, and Bao Du King too shabby. They had tried to close it down. When the newspapers printed the story, Bao Du King became famous.

Mei had come because she believed Bao Du King might lead her to someone who knew about the paper butterfly. He had lived in the neighbourhood for almost half a century and knew its residents well. Also, elderly residents gathered at his restaurant for a taste of old Beijing and to meet each other.

Mei was confident that Bao Du King would know if the paper butterfly was indeed from here.

Presently a small wrinkled woman came out from the back. She wore a black knitted hat over white hair. Her face had begun to sink in the middle – her eyes, nose and mouth seemed to be falling into a hole. She brought Mei tea and smiled toothlessly. Mei remembered that Bao Du King ran the restaurant with his wife.

Soon, he emerged with a dish of boiled lamb tripe buried under a thick sesame sauce.

"When did *bao du* come to Beijing?" asked Mei, when he set down the bowl.

"You don't know?" said Bao Du King, incredulously. "More than a hundred years ago Emperor Qianlong led a campaign in the Western Region. The army ran out of food. Desperate, the royal cook boiled the tripe of a dead cow for the emperor, who thought it was the best meal he'd ever had. After the war had been won, the emperor came back to Beijing and ordered the dish again. That's why we have our famous *bao du*."

The two elderly men had finished their lunch. They picked their teeth with their fingernails. Then one cursed and got up. They shouted to Bao Du King that they were leaving. He ran to them. "Sit a little longer!"

"We're going."

"Walk slowly."

"It's cold!"

Mrs Bao Du came out of the kitchen with a large bowl of food in each hand and put them on a table in the corner. Bao

Du King went over and sat down. They exchanged a few words and began their lunch.

Mei thought her chance had come and approached them.

"Big Papa, Big Mama, I'm sorry to trouble you." She took a carefully wrapped parcel from her bag, then showed them the white paper butterfly. "I believe this came from somewhere near here. Do you know anything about it? Who made them?"

Bao Du King and his wife gazed at the paper butterfly, then at each other. Bao Du King picked it up and turned it over. "Are you looking for more of these?" he asked.

Mei sat at their table. "Maybe. What are they for?"

"You burn them. They're for funerals, a Manchu custom."

"Like ghost money."

"Yes. It was the custom in the Qing emperor's time, with the royal court being Manchu, but we Han Chinese didn't do it." He frowned. "Where did you find it? I haven't seen one for years."

"It came from a friend."

"Your friend should know who made it."

"I'm afraid she can't tell me."

"Why not?"

"She's dead."

Bao Du King looked at his wife. "Big Papa Liu," she said.

Bao Du King nodded. "He's a travelling barber. He's lived here even longer than I have, and has been cutting hair in the neighbouring *hutongs* for decades. He's seventy-six but still goes out every day to see his customers." He cleared his throat. "He'd be the one to ask. He's superstitious – he believes in demons, the afterlife, such things ..."

"Where can I find him?"

"At this hour, it's hard to say. He might be at home. He lives in Tofu Mill Hutong."

"Number nineteen," said Mrs Bao Du, and gave Mei directions.

Mei thanked them, paid for her *bao du* and dry-baked buns, then left. The sky was tinted with the blue mist of early evening. A slender crescent moon rose above Silver Ingot Bridge.

Mei crossed the bridge and took a right turn into a wide alley where a man was flipping baked yams on a barrel stove. Further down a woman was selling steamed buns. An old man rummaged through early editions in a small bookstore. The bell clanged in the Bell Tower.

Inside the *hutong*, children played noisily, chasing each other. Adults cycled in, on their way home from work. Mei made another right turn into Tofu Mill Hutong at a corner shop. A group of boys were playing football,.

A strange, sad sight greeted her at number nineteen. Two large white lanterns, signifying a death in the household, swayed above the entrance, like the wandering eyes of a ghost. A couple of old women chatted at the gate while the children they were minding played with the snow.

"Are you looking for someone in particular?" one asked Mei suspiciously.

"Big Papa Liu."

She snorted. "He's gone out."

"Do you know where he went?"

"The *qipei* room."

"Does he really play cards every day?" asked her friend.

"That *qipei* room has corrupted even good family men."

"Can you tell me where it is?" asked Mei.

They each raised an arm, pointing in opposite directions, and said, "That way."

It took Mei some time to find the *qipei* room because it had no sign and resembled any other street-fronted house in a residential lane. It was smoky, smelled of alcohol, and was filled with people playing cards, Chinese chess, *go* and mahjong.

The proprietor, Old Big as people called him, came towards Mei aggressively when she entered, perhaps fearing that she was from the district inspection bureau. But when Mei told him who she was looking for, he pointed to a corner table where two old men were playing cards.

One had white hair and curved lips, while the other was skinny, with jet black hair cut very short. He had a small mole near his nose, which sprouted a long hair. A bottle of *er-guo-tuo*, rice wine spirit, stood between them on the table.

Mei walked over and heard the white-haired man saying, "I heard Grandpa Wu passed away. What happened?"

The man with the mole answered, in a high-pitched voice, "Old age. The wife of Cop Chen found him dead in the morning after the snow."

"Another gone. Soon we'll all be dead," hissed the other man. "How old was he?"

"He was four years older than we are, so he was eighty."

"A long life."

"But a sad one."

They sighed and went on with their game.

"Big Papa Liu?" Mei called.

Both men looked up. "What do you want with him?" said the man with the mole.

Mei took off her long black coat and her black woollen hat, then sat down. She smiled, her lips the same shade as her pink sweater. "Bao Du King told me you might look at something for me."

"What is it?"

Mei took out the packet and unwrapped it.

Big Papa Liu gave a tiny shriek. "Where did you get this?"

"It's mine," said Mei, puzzled.

"Liu, are you all right?" the white-haired man leaned forward.

"Who are you?" Big Papa Liu's face had turned pale. The cards slipped from his fingers.

The white-haired man poured *er-guo-tuo* into a cup and handed it to his friend who drank it in one gulp. He asked for a refill and swallowed that too. His eyes darted from Mei to the butterfly, then back to Mei. Others turned their heads, wondering what the commotion was about.

"This is too strange!" Big Papa Liu shook his head. He gestured for another shot. The bottle was empty. Mei bought another from the proprietor. "But Grandpa Wu is dead!" He kept on saying.

Two more cups later, he seemed to calm down.

"Did Grandpa Wu make paper butterflies?" Mei ventured.

"Yes. It was his family trade. They were Manchu. In the old days they supplied the royal court." His voice sounded like that of a small animal trapped in a dark tunnel. "Years ago they had a little shop of funeral supplies, but it was destroyed in the Smash Four Olds Movement." He drank another shot of *er-guo-tuo* and the colour returned to his face. "After that, there were no more burials, and the traditions that went with them were banned. Chairman Mao said they were superstitious rituals.

"We thought that was the end. But then came the Cultural Revolution. One night the Red Guards came to our *hutong* and smashed up the Wu family house. They burned all the paper butterflies. I'd told Grandpa Wu to get rid of them. 'Don't keep them in your house,' I said to him. 'Look, you were Manchu *and* you trade in superstitious rituals.' But he didn't understand the danger. He was too old and the baby was too young, so the Red Guards took away his son and daughter-in-law. The next day they were dead, skulls cracked, faces smashed. Grandpa Wu had to collect their bodies. They'd been dumped on the street where they'd died. After that, he stopped making paper butterflies. He wouldn't even talk about it."

"But how did he make a living?" Mei asked.

"He cleaned the streets and the local schools. He was a caretaker. He brought up his grandson on his own."

"Where is the grandson now?"

"No one knows."

"What's his name?"

"Lin."

That's it! thought Mei. Lin must be L. The name fits. The place fits. His grandpa was a caretaker at the local school and that fits too.

Mei picked up the butterfly and tried to give it to Big Papa Liu. But he wouldn't touch it.

"How can you be sure that this is one of Grandpa Wu's butterflies? There must be others who can make them."

"It's Grandpa Wu's. We've lived in the same *hutong* for more than seventy years and I'd have recognised it anywhere. This is a Wu family butterfly. The golden veins were their specialty."

"There you are." The white-haired man grinned. "What are you frightened of? It's only Grandpa Wu's butterfly."

"Didn't you hear me? Grandpa Wu is dead. A dead man can't make paper butterflies."

"Perhaps he made this one long before he died, many years ago," said Mei.

"But did he make all the others too?"

"What others?"

"The day after Grandpa Wu died, there was a paper butterfly on the doorstep of each house in the courtyard."

"What are you talking about?" Mei was bewildered.

"His spirit is haunting us!"

"You're being superstitious again," said the white-haired man. "Besides, you were Grandpa Wu's friend for sixty years. You've nothing to worry about from his ghost."

"You never know – maybe he didn't like the storage hut I built on to the back of his house. But everyone was taking space for himself. If I hadn't, someone else would have. Perhaps he didn't like my gossiping. But we all looked after him. I did his shopping and Mrs Tang, who used to be the chairwoman of our Street and Hutong Revolutionary Committee, collected his retirement money for him. Mrs Chen cooked for him. He couldn't have had better neighbours."

The white-haired man nodding.

"Grandpa Wu had no relatives," Big Papa Liu went on. "Cop Chen took his body to the crematorium. These days, it's expensive to cremate a body. Tomorrow we'll have a wake for him. All the old neighbours will be there."

"I'll come," said the white-haired man.

Big Papa Liu stopped talking, his eyes dim. The hair in his mole quivered. His fingers trembled as he tried to touch the paper butterfly lying on the table. "Spirits work in mysterious ways," he murmured.

The white-haired man grabbed his arm. "There *are* no spirits. That's superstition. Haven't the Communists taught you anything?"

"You say so, but what about the pig's ears hanging over your door? Tell me you don't believe in demons," Big Papa Liu retorted.

24

The next morning Mei telephoned the Ministry of Posts and Telecommunications to talk to Jing Jing, the little sister of Big Sister Hui, Mei's best friend from university. In contrast to her plump sibling, Jing Jing was as skinny as a stick and had a voice to match.

"How odd that you've called," said Jing Jing, in her sing-song voice. "We were talking about you the other day."

"Really?"

"My sister thinks she's found someone for you."

"Again?"

Jing Jing giggled. "She feels bad about the last one. Who'd have known he'd be so awful? This one is just the opposite. He's not much to look at but very nice. Why not call her? The university broke up for the winter break two weeks ago and she's bored at home."

"I thought she was writing a collection of poems."

"I don't think it's going very well. But don't tell her I said that. You *must* phone her," Jing Jing pleaded. "She's knitting hats for us again."

"And organising my love life," said Mei.

They laughed.

Then Mei gave Jing Jing Kaili's mobile phone number. "Can you give me a list of calls made from it over the last six months? I know you're busy, but it's important."

"I may not get round to it until tomorrow."

"That's fine. By the way, when's the reorganisation?"

"How did you know about that? It's supposed to be a secret."

"That's why everyone knows."

"After the New Year and it'll be ugly," Jing Jing said. Then: "My boss is coming. I'd better go."

After they'd hung up Mei tried to fill in some forms that had arrived from the city government, but she was preoccupied with the mystery of the paper butterfly. Why had there been one for each neighbour? How had they got there? Why were they so frightened? Mei was sure now that L was Lin, Grandpa Wu's grandson. She thought of Kaili. Why had she made those visits to the Drum Tower area?

There was a noodle bar round the corner that she liked so she picked up her coat and was about to go out when she heard a knock at the door.

Two bulky men in down jackets stood outside. One carried a briefcase.

"Are you Mei Wang?"

"Yes," Mei answered reluctantly.

"We're from the Bureau of Regulation."

Without waiting for permission, they entered and took off their jackets. They pulled up a couple of chairs and sat down next to each other.

Mei sat down too. "What's this about?"

The man with the briefcase opened it and took out a folder. "You're the owner of Lotus Information Consultancy, located at 122 Building No. 1, Red Scarf Commune, Chongyang North Road. You currently have one employee, a migrant worker from Henan. Are these details correct?"

"Yes." Mei had a feeling that the conversation was about to take a nasty turn.

"We have recently discovered that some people use legal companies like yours as a front for illegal activities such as private investigation. We need to see your books to make sure you've been operating in accordance with the law and regulations."

"Has someone informed on me? Am I being investigated?"

"We are also missing a few forms from you, the Declaration of Spirit Cleanliness, Form 11956, Form 20010, et cetera. Do you know that it's illegal to run a business without having filed Form 11956? We might have to ask you to stop trading for a while until we have received all the required documents and are satisfied with them."

Mei didn't know what Form 11956 was or whether it existed. But she had no doubt that if the bureau wanted to, it could shut her down tomorrow. She had always been aware the risk. But unless the government instigated it, crackdowns like this were rare. After all, hundreds if not thousands of private investigators operated successfully under the umbrella of information consultants – she had met them at their annual conference. Why should she be singled out?

The other man, who had not said a word so far, shifted in his seat, crossing his legs. "Mr Peng has been generous and patient, but you are still working on Kaili's case. He's upset."

"If you stop," said the man with the briefcase, "we might be able to overlook the missing forms – for now."

The other man stood up. He walked into Mei's office, nodded at Mei's mother's paintings hanging on the wall and stroked her computer. "You have a nice business. I'm sure you want to protect it. Mr Peng is doing the same thing," he said, rather quietly, as if he was begging Mei to understand.

After they had left, Mei paced up and down her office, her heart beating rapidly. If she didn't stop probing Kaili's death, they might be back to carry out their threat. But if she stopped now, no one would ever know the truth about Kaili or Lin. Would she be able to live with herself if she yielded to a man like Mr Peng?

A ray of sunshine poured through the window on to her mother's painting of a single lotus flower rising from mud. What would her father have done? she asked herself silently.

She smiled and felt a renewed energy. She remembered the day on which she had handed in her resignation to the ministry, her strength and dignity. She would follow her heart. She would not be bullied. She would neither give in nor give up.

⁊

Slow, eerie *erhu* music drifted out of No. 19 Tofu Mill Hutong. It made Mei feel sad, yet drew her in. The gate clattered in the wind. Mei pulled it open and walked through. The first house of the courtyard was open and lit by candlelight. Mei went in.

The house had only one room, about seven metres long and three wide. The ceiling was low, and an altar stood by the back wall, white candles and incense burning on it. Pictures hung on the wall above a single bed. Some had frames, others were secured with drawing-pins. They were all of one person. There he was a boy, wearing a red scarf and showing off a Three-Good Award. There he was again, a few years older, grinning beside a new bicycle. More pictures showed him as a young man, standing by the sea, clear-eyed and handsome. Mei guessed that he was Lin.

A group of people, all wearing black armbands, sat near the altar. The *erhu* player was an ancient man with a long silver beard. A plump middle-aged woman sat next to him. As soon as she saw Mei come in, she wailed loudly. Mei guessed that she was a professional mourner. Next to her, a young monk chanted his rosary, unfazed.

The last of the group was a young woman. She had a round face and gentle eyes. Her hair was tied up in a bun. Fire burned in an aluminium washing basin in front of her, and from time to time she dropped in a handful of white ghost money.

Mei walked up to the altar and bowed before the picture of the dead man. She lit an incense stick and added it to the others.

The mourner wailed again. Mei turned. An elderly couple had walked into the room, holding on to each other for support. The mourner waved her handkerchief and cried, "His Grandpa!"

The couple shuffled towards the altar. The old man wavered, his face crumpled like a walnut. At the altar the woman bowed while the man managed only a jerk of his head. The young woman who was burning ghost money came to help them. The old couple offered their condolences. Mei wondered who the young woman was. She moved towards the altar, thinking to offer her own prayers, but the woman stopped her with a gesture.

"Please go into the courtyard for the wake," she said.

Mei nodded.

The night had turned cold. Mei pulled her coat tightly round her. She could hardly see the path. Extensions, rickety huts and storage sheds formed dark shapes in the gloom. A maple tree rose high above them, hands reaching to the sky.

Further on, Mei heard voices and saw shadows moving inside a house. She went in. The room was crowded. A group of women sat at the edge of a bed, cracking roasted watermelon seeds, heaps of empty shells at their feet. Men crowded round a card table, smoking and drinking rice wine. A *mahjong* table had been set up in a corner. Roasted peanuts and dried dates were being passed round. Everyone in the room was dressed in dull clothes and wore black armbands.

Big Papa Liu was there, watching a game of *mahjong*. His face contorted when he saw Mei. He lowered his head, pretending he hadn't noticed her.

"*Ayi*, would you like a sweet?" a child's voice said. Mei lowered her eyes and saw a little girl of about five holding a small basket. She had large eyes, rosy cheeks and a dimple at one corner of her mouth. Her hair had been plaited into two pigtails, which were fastened with black ribbons.

Mei knelt down and took a sweet from the basket. "Thank you. What's your name?"

"Chen Xiao Hua," said the child, shyly, each word more muted than the last.

"Little Flower. That's a pretty name."

Little Flower stared at Mei, then ran away.

A woman in her fifties came up to Mei. "That's Cop Chen's little girl."

Mei's eyes followed Little Flower to her father, a lean young man who was talking loudly and drinking rice wine at the card table.

"I'm Mrs Tang. Have I seen you before? You look familiar."

"You've mistaken me for someone else," Mei said. "Tonight is the first time I've been here. I'm a friend of Lin, Grandpa Wu's grandson."

"Friend? To that not-worth-a-breath turtle's egg?" Mrs Tang exclaimed. She spat out the empty shell of a watermelon seed. "Grandpa Wu worked day and night to send him to university, and what did he do? He turned against the Party. It broke the old man's heart. He couldn't believe his grandson would do something like that, not till the day he died." She shook her head.

Mrs Tang had high cheekbones and a splayed nose. Her lips were thin and pressed together. Clearly her mouth was used to uttering harsh words. This was accentuated by her posture: she stood with her back straight and her legs apart in a masculine stance. Dressed from head to toe in black, she seemed to be the matriarch of the wake.

Mrs Tang opened her left fist and offered Mei a few roasted watermelon seeds. "*Guazi?*"

Mei took one and thanked her. "Have you lived here long?" she asked.

"More than thirty years," said Mrs Tang proudly. "I used to be the chairwoman of the Street and Hutong Revolutionary Committee, but I'm retired now. Come with me," she said, grabbing Mei's arm and leading her to the bed. "The female comrades are over here."

Mei followed, empty shells cracking under her feet as she sat on the edge of the bed. From the corner of her eye, she saw Big Papa Liu peering covertly at her. He was talking to Little Flower's father, Cop Chen.

"What happened to the body?" asked a woman with fizzy permed hair.

"Cop Chen took care of it," answered Mrs Tang.

"So soon after the death?"

"Grandpa Wu had no family. It was good of him to pay for the cremation."

"Wasn't Chen a friend of the grandson at one time?" said another woman, with bulging goldfish eyes.

"They'd been close since they were small. They used to climb that old tree in the yard. I had to scold them. Lin was the clever one." Mrs Tang cracked a seed with her teeth.

"How is Cop Chen doing, these days?"

"He's with the great man himself. Imagine! He takes charge of President Li Peng's daily travel."

The goldfish-eyed woman sniggered. Mrs Tang turned. Cop Chen had swaggered over to them with a cigarette between his fingers. "Ladies, Mrs Tang." He nodded.

"Is the silver Volkswagen parked outside the courtyard yours?" asked the woman with the perm.

"Yes. 150 horse-power, 5000 r.p.m., turbo."

The women giggled, not understanding.

"We've never met. I'm Chen Xiaolei. People here call me Cop Chen." He held out his hand to Mei. She shook it. "Mei Wang."

"She's a friend of Lin," said Mrs Tang.

"Are you?" Cop Chen shifted his feet. "He and I were childhood friends."

"Are you Fatty?"

The colour left his face, "I hated that nickname," he muttered. "How did you know Lin?" he asked, drawing on his cigarette, then letting out a lungful of smoke.

A loud wail soared outside, announcing a new arrival to the altar room.

"University," said Mei.

Cop Chen stared at her. Mei knew that she had sounded as if she was lying. "But you're a Beijinger."

The door opened, letting in a cold draught. Someone very old, very small, very dry and fragile was being helped into the room.

"Old Mrs Guo!" exclaimed Mrs Tang. She pushed past everyone to take the old woman's arm.

People stood up, murmuring.

"I haven't seen her for years."

"I didn't know she was still alive."

"I didn't know she could walk."

"Not for long, they say. She's eighty-eight."

"They say she's as deaf as a post."

Mrs Tang and the young woman who had been burning ghost money in the altar room half lifted and half dragged Old Mrs Guo to the card table. People rushed over to her – women wanted to touch her for luck. Mrs Tang shouted to her husband, a tiny man in a corner, to bring *ju hua* – chrysanthemum-flower tea.

One person didn't stir. Cop Chen stood apart from the scene and watched. A little later, the young woman from the altar room slipped across to him and whispered in his ear. Mei saw her peering in her direction.

Mrs Tang cleared her throat. "Old Mrs Guo, it's an honour to have you in my home."

"I came to say goodbye to Grandpa Wu." The old lady's voice was surprisingly clear.

The evening went on. People became drunk and rowdy. The sound of *mahjong* tiles sliding on the table rose above a sea of noise to echo under the low ceiling. Old Mrs Guo, who had gone to sleep, was snoring. Eventually she was carried out of the room and the party ended.

25

Outside No. 19 Tofu Mill Hutong, a few stars twinkled in the cold winter sky. In the distance, the Drum Tower loomed like a phantom. Mei took a flashlight out of her handbag and switched it on. Snow lay at the bottom of the alleyway. The *hutong* twisted and turned. Her footsteps echoed between the dark walls.

At the end of Tofu Mill Hutong, there was a crossroads. A shop stood beneath a skeletal tree, its door shut. She turned into another alley. There, she heard footsteps other than her own. She switched off the flashlight and the darkness closed in on her.

Panicking, she began to walk very fast. Another *hutong* emerged, veering this way and that. In the dark it was like a maze. Everything looked recognisable – ramshackle huts and peeling walls – yet nothing was familiar. Where was the way out? She looked around desperately. The Drum Tower that had been on the right had moved to the left.

At the top of a *hutong*, Mei stopped. She took a deep breath of cold air and let her thoughts wash over her.

Whoever was following her must have realised that she was lost, but hadn't approached. Mei swallowed. She was not in immediate danger of attack. Her stalker was following her for a reason.

Mei began to walk, keeping an eye on the Drum Tower. She took her time. Ten minutes later, she could see the faint glow of street-lamps. She walked towards them and was soon out of the *hutong* on Drum Tower West Street.

A few cyclists pedalled past, their faces hidden under winter hats. A night bus purred along. Mei saw her car on the other side of the road.

She ran up the street and turned back into the *hutong*. She waited in the dark. Time trickled by. Then she saw, outlined by the dim street-lamps, Cop Chen darting up and down, searching. At last he went towards the Drum Tower.

With her flashlight still off, Mei stumbled through the *hutong*. When one alleyway ended, another began. At a corner, she bumped into a bicycle that had been left leaning against the wall. Slowly her eyes adjusted and she saw the vague shapes of abandoned chairs, rubbish heaps and the tin roofs of home extensions.

A few turnings later, she was back at Tofu Mill Hutong. As before, the white lanterns swayed above the entrance to No. 19. Mei gave the half-open gate a little push. It squeaked. A dim light died inside Grandpa Wu's house.

Mei flung open the door. She turned on her flashlight and pointed it into the dark room. Big Papa Liu's frightened eyes stared back. "What are you doing?" she snapped.

"Ssh. Let's not talk here," Big Papa Liu mumbled. "Turn off your flashlight, please."

Mei didn't move.

"Someone will see us!" he hissed. "Please, I beg you, come to my house. I'll tell you everything."

Mei peered at his face with the mole. Her eyes narrowed. Could she trust him? She switched off the flashlight.

Outside Grandpa Wu's house, Big Papa Liu locked the door. "He gave me the key. He was sick and I looked after him," he explained.

They went to the back of the courtyard and the smallest house. A tricycle, its handlebars twisted at a curious angle, was parked beneath the window. Big Papa Liu hurried Mei inside.

He pulled a string and a bulb in the middle of the ceiling lit the room. Furniture was piled at both sides of the door. Cardboard boxes, washing basins, bowls and cooking pots were jumbled on top of a chest and on the floor. The room smelled of pickled *tofu*.

Big Papa Liu swept a mound of objects off a chair to the floor. A dozen dried plums spilled out of a bag.

Mei moved to the chair, the only one in the room.

"No!" he exclaimed. "You can't sit here. It's bad luck."

He carried the chair to the end of the room and turned it to face the door. "Sit here," he said. "I'll take the bed."

The bed filled the entire back wall. A small table stood beside it, with old newspapers, glass jars, teacups and a brick-sized cooking knife covering its surface. Big Papa Liu scrabbled among the confusion for a packet of cigarettes. When he found one, he shuffled everything around again, searching for a box of matches.

"What were you looking for in Grandpa Wu's house?"

Big Papa Liu pushed the quilts to the corner of the bed and sat down. "I wasn't looking for anything. I was returning things."

"What things?"

He puffed his cigarette. "Money. I'm not a thief, if that's what you're thinking. I'd never dishonour Grandpa Wu. He was my friend for sixty years. But why let money rot under the mattress? Or, worse, let someone else find it? I've looked after him for years. I deserve compensation."

"How much money?"

"Thousands of yuan. Lin's friend gave it to him. He didn't want it but she insisted. I told Grandpa Wu she must have been a girlfriend, or why would she come to see him and give him money? He said she was rich."

"How many times did she come?"

"Two or three times, and each time he was upset. He didn't like talking about Lin."

"What happened to Lin?"

Big Papa Liu took the cigarette out of his mouth. "I thought you were his friend."

"I've never met him."

"But Cop Chen thought you were …" He stopped, gazing at the window.

Mei listened. The night was quiet, but for the hum of the lightbulb overhead. "What did he say?"

Big Papa Liu fidgeted, twisting the cigarette between his fingers. Mei remembered what he had said at the *qipei* room about his gossiping. Gossips love to have a secret to tell.

"He said you were with him. He said you're in touch with Lin."

"What made him think that?"

Big Papa Liu's expression was grave. "The paper butterflies."

That explained why Chen had followed her, thought Mei. But what had he meant by 'in touch with him'? Did he think she would lead him to Lin?

"Do you know who I am?" Mei decided to be straight with Big Papa Liu. He was a superstitious gossip and might be just the person to help her prise open the secret.

He stared at her intently. "Grandpa Wu's spirit is upset. First came the paper butterflies, then you. You're his messenger. Tonight when I saw you at Mrs Tang's, I decided I had to return the money. I *kowtow*ed to Grandpa Wu and begged his forgiveness."

"You think I'm a spirit?"

"No. But you're a sign. There's no such thing as coincidence. Everything happens for a reason."

"I agree with you there, but I'm not Grandpa Wu's messenger. I'm here to solve the mystery of the paper butterflies. Like you, I want to find out where they came from and who made them." Mei handed him a business card. "My job is to solve people's problems."

Big Papa Liu read the card, but he seemed unconvinced.

"You can't believe that the paper butterflies were placed by Grandpa Wu's spirit," said Mei.

"I do."

"Then you believe it because you have no alternative explanation. Let me find out. I can help you."

Big Papa Liu puffed his cigarette, then blew smoke. He looked uncertain.

"But for me to help you, you must tell me what you know," Mei persisted. "The more, the better."

"What do you want to know?"

"Everything. First, what did Grandpa Wu tell you about Lin's old girlfriend?"

"It was a few months ago. He said a friend of Lin's from university had come to see him. It was odd that she'd come now after so many years, he said. Then she came a couple more times and brought money. I suppose she felt sorry for him. Grandpa Wu had been ill since the weather had turned cold. He didn't want the money but she left it anyway."

"What else?"

"He said she was sorry it had taken her so long to come. She asked about Lin. But, of course, Grandpa Wu hadn't had any news since Lin was arrested. That was ... nine years ago."

"Why was he arrested?"

"June the fourth. The foolish boy went to Tiananmen Square. He must have gone at night without telling anyone. When he came back the next day, he was talking blood and death. Whatever happened out there hit him hard. We told him to keep quiet, but he went back — every day. He said he wanted to help — we didn't know who. Soldiers patrolled the streets. Grandpa Wu was very worried. He was afraid Lin would be arrested and not come back.

"One night, the police raided this courtyard. It was past midnight and I was asleep. By the time I came out, they'd taken Lin away. Grandpa Wu went mad. Seventy-one years old with a walking-stick, he went everywhere trying to find news of his grandson. A few months later we heard that Lin had been sentenced to ten years hard labour. That was the last we heard of him. Grandpa Wu fell ill. His health worsened with every year that passed. At the end, he was mostly bed-bound. The neighbours cared for him."

"When did he die?"

"We think it was the night of the blizzard. Mrs Chen found his body the next morning. She said he had died in peace. He even looked happy. The poor man had a tough life. Every year we thought he'd not get through winter, but he did, sadder than a ghost.

"The evening after he died, the neighbours met at Cop Chen's home. He said he would take the body to the crematorium. The next morning I got up to fetch water from the tap in the yard and a paper butterfly was lying in the snow by my door. You can imagine my fright."

Big Papa Liu extinguished his cigarette on the sole of his shoe and threw the stub on to the floor. "I was so upset that I went straight over to Grandpa Wu's house to check he was really dead. I told Mrs Chen about it. She works half-day shifts at the Long Fu supermarket. She said they'd had one too. We went to see Mrs Tang. She'd had one but she thought it was a joke. She said my superstitious thoughts were stupid and I shouldn't believe in ghosts."

"What did Cop Chen say about the butterfly?"

"He was very short-tempered, and thought I was talking nonsense about spirits."

"But I said to them, 'We're old neighbours. We must have a wake for Grandpa Wu or his spirit will always be angry with us and never go away.' Cop Chen agreed, but said he didn't believe in superstition. Mrs Tang said it was all nonsense but insisted on hosting the party." Big Papa Liu swallowed. "Now that we've had the wake and I've returned the money, I hope his spirit will be appeased." He took out another cigarette and looked about for the matchbox.

"Did you see anything suspicious when you found the paper butterfly, like footprints?" Mei asked.

"I was in such a panic when I ran to Grandpa Wu's house that if there were any footprints I'd have ruined them."

"Did anyone else know he had money?"

"I might have told Mrs Chen. I'm such a gossip. Sometimes I want to slap my own face. But no one else knew where he hid the money. I doubt that the Chens would want it anyway. Cop Chen does pretty well for himself."

Big Papa Liu paused, eyes flashing. "You don't suppose someone's after it?"

Mei looked at her watch. It was past midnight. "Thank you. I'll come again," she said.

Big Papa Liu got to his feet. "I cut people's hair. There isn't much money in it. These days, the young people want to go to modern salons. I don't have children. When I'm old and can't work, who will look after me? I'm not a thief."

Mei stopped at the door. She had walked on something soft and squashed it. She looked down and saw a dried plum.

26

The next day a long fax from Jing Jing and a note from Gupin were waiting for Mei when she went into her office. She read Gupin's message first. "Well done!" she said aloud, and smiled.

Jing Jing's fax was a list of calls from Kaili's mobile phone. Mei took the pages to her desk, copied some numbers on to a clean piece of paper, ticked off, tallied and crossed out. In the end she found three numbers that Kaili had called frequently before she disappeared. Two were mobile numbers. She checked her address book and found, as she had expected, that one was Mr Peng's. She called the second. Out of service. The third was for a land line. The phone rang twice and a young female voice answered: "Huan Chun lawyers, good morning."

"Good morning. My name is Mei Wang. I run a small information consultancy. I may need legal representation."

"Would you like to speak to one of our partners?" asked the pretty voice.

"Yes, please"

A few minutes later, a man spoke.

"A friend of mine used your firm," Mei told him. "Do you know Kaili, the pop singer? I would like to talk to her lawyer. She told me his name, but I've forgotten it."

The man went off to check. Mei waited.

He came back a few minutes later. "She was with Lawyer Li Bo. Unfortunately he is in a meeting at the moment. May I ask him to call you once he's free?"

"I'll ring later," said Mei.

After they had hung up, Mei dialled Detective Zhao.

"I've no use for information now," Detective Zhao said grumpily. "District took on Kaili's case, but when I spoke to an old friend from the academy, he told me it wasn't to be investigated any further. I underestimated Mr Peng's power."

"I'm not giving up. You shouldn't either. For every boss, there's a higher boss. Who's to say District has the last word? Whether it wants the case investigated or not, if you solve it there will still be credit, especially when you arrest the culprit."

"But I've no support," said Detective Zhao.

"We can work together, but we must cast our net carefully. It will be difficult but it's worth a try." She paused, then went on, "I think I've found out something that might be useful, but I need your help."

Detective Zhao didn't say anything.

Mei imagined him weighing up his options. "You're not going to let Mr Peng have his way, are you?"

"How can I help?" said the detective at last.

"My assistant found out that a migrant worker has gone missing from Factory 958. He might be the man you're looking for. They call him Little Gansu. Can you get a description of him and perhaps even a photo? I have here a few names of people who will talk to you."

Mei read the names off Gupin's note for Detective Zhao to take down. Then she told him about Lawyer Li. "I'd like to know what Kaili wanted with him. He probably won't tell me but he'll have no choice if you ask him."

"I'll see them this afternoon."

They said goodbye and Mei dialled another number.

"The Ministry for Public Security," said a woman.

Mei gave an extension number. The phone rang for a long time before someone picked it up. "Hello?" said a sleepy voice.

"Is that Yang Chao?"

"Yes." He was suddenly awake.

"This is Mei Wang, your old colleague from Public Relations."

"Mei!" he exclaimed. "How are you? I heard you'd gone private, set up your own business. How is it going? You've really shown those cunning ghost faces." Chao uttered a string of curses. "I'm sorry I haven't been in touch. I meant to phone you." He was among the very few at the ministry who had supported Mei during the campaign organised against her by her boss that had eventually led her to resign.

"I didn't call either," said Mei.

"It was my fault. I shouldn't have let my ex-girlfriend bully me," said Chao.

Mei remembered her: she had pencilled in her eyebrows and worn a lot of other makeup. She had watched Mei intently from behind a pair of spectacles with thin wire frames.

"When did you two break up?"

"Seven months ago. It's for the best. We never really got on. I think in the end she became disappointed with my career prospects. Since you left I've hardly advanced in the department. But things are changing. The old man's retiring."

Mei felt a thrill run through her body like an electric current. Her former boss was going.

"It's really good to hear from you," said Chao, "but I suppose you didn't call just to say hello. How can I help?"

Mei smiled. On one hand she was embarrassed by his frankness, but on the other, she was pleasantly surprised by his easy-going, no-nonsense approach. He had changed, thought Mei. The image of a twenty-two-year-old headstrong young man rearranged itself in her mind.

"Could you run checks on two people for me?" She gave him the names of Lin and Cop Chen and told him their story.

"I'll do my best. How soon do you need the results?"

"The sooner the better."

"How late can I call?"

"Any time," said Mei.

27

Pigeons cooed inside rusty cages above the roofs of the courtyard houses. Two hundred yards away from the Street and Hutong Revolutionary Committee office, gambling addicts sneaked into yet another hidden *qipei* room. A young woman poked her head out of a door. Then, seeing only Mei, she poured a basin of dirty water beside a communal wall on which a notice had been painted: "Dumping Is Strictly Forbidden."

Bicycle rickshaw tours whistled past, bells ringing. Old women walked up the *hutong*, heaving shopping baskets. On the surface everything seemed as normal. Then a group of middle-aged women rushed down the passage, muttering to each other, and Mei noticed something strange. Neighbours gathered outside their courtyard gates, heads together, expressions anxious. Children were being summoned home. Then Mei heard voices rippling down frozen alleyways.

"Gone? What do you mean?"

"Disappeared. It was all in ten minutes, they say. She was

playing in her *hutong*. When her mother came out to get her, she'd gone."

"Which Little Flower?"

"Mother Chen's, the one with pigtails."

"The committee's organising a search."

"Ming Ming, go home!"

Mei stopped. Little Flower, gone, disappeared …

They saw Mei. "What do you want?" shouted a freckled woman in a padded grey jacket.

Mei shook her head and hurried off. Behind her, she heard suspicious whispers.

At the top of the *hutong*, the alley curved and widened. She found herself in front of the corner shop. She bought two packs of Spring Festival firecrackers. "Have you heard about Cop Chen's little daughter?" she asked.

"Can't believe it," said the shopkeeper, picking up a half-smoked cigarette and stuffing it between his lips.

"You don't think …" Mei tailed off deliberately.

He nodded gravely. "You often hear of little boys being kidnapped and sold to rich families who want a son, but they never seem to take girls. Many neighbours have gone out to look for her."

"You think they'll find her?"

The shopkeeper shook his head.

"Someone must have seen something," said Mei.

"There are strangers everywhere, these days. Ever since they redeveloped Houhai, we've had all sorts hanging about. You never know who's good and who's bad."

"Maybe she's lost."

"She was playing outside her own courtyard. She knows the *hutong*. She couldn't get lost. Cop Chen's already gone to the station."

Mei said goodbye and walked towards Tofu Mill Hutong.

The gate at number nineteen stood wide. Mei entered. A ghostly silence reigned in the courtyard. Grandpa Wu's house was padlocked. The little hut under the maple tree, which the Chens had added a few years ago as a kitchen, was dark. The coal stove had not been lit.

The door to Cop Chen's house was ajar. Mei pushed it open. Two of the women from last night were there, holding towels. Mrs Tang sat at the table saying something urgently, in a muted voice. Her tiny husband stood in a corner, his face shadowed.

Abruptly Mrs Chen turned. Her eyes lit for a second, then darkened again. Tears fell.

Mei closed the door behind her.

"Sister Chen, don't cry. We'll find her," said the woman with permed hair. She offered her a towel, but Mrs Chen didn't move.

"The police will," said the goldfish-eyed woman.

Mrs Chen shrieked. The word "police" seemed to have touched a nerve. Police involvement meant accepting that her daughter had been kidnapped. Clearly the very idea broke her heart.

The door burst open. Big Papa Liu darted in. "I heard about Little Flower at Old Fang's. Is it true?"

Mrs Tang nodded grimly.

"It's heaven's punishment!" he shrieked.

"Nonsense!" snapped Mrs Tang.

"You know what I'm talking about."

"And I know that you're a superstitious old fool. But spirits and ghosts are anti-revolutionary."

Mr Tang emerged from the shadows and brought Big Papa Liu a chair. The old man shook his head. "All of you," he wagged a shaking finger and stared at them crazily. "Don't you see? It's heaven's revenge." He pointed at the ceiling.

"Go home, Liu. You need rest." Mrs Tang's voice was icy cold.

Mrs Chen had stopped crying. The two neighbourhood women took his arms, uttering soothing words, their voices washing over his hysteria like the clucking of a hen. Mr Tang shouted something. Big Papa Liu tried to break free and backed into the table, knocking a cup of hot tea over Mrs Chen. She screamed.

Amid the commotion, Mrs Tang stood motionless, her lips pressed together, eyes glazed.

It took a while to quieten Big Papa Liu. Gradually he ceased shaking and his eyes steadied. He gave a low moan, then he picked up his hairdressing bag, which he had dropped at the door when he came in, and left.

"What could have got into him?" said the goldfish-eyed woman.

Mrs Tang cut her off with a wave of her hand. "Chairman Mao was right. People from the old society are dangerous.

They can't be reformed. The Communist Party has tried. We've tried. I've spent thirty years dealing with such people." The former Street and Hutong Revolutionary Committee chairwoman glowed with resolve.

Mei knew people like Mrs Tang. Communism was their life. In their world, people belonged to one of two camps: revolutionary and anti-revolutionary. Mei had always found it odd that her mother's generation should have such a blind faith in the system. The more they suffered, the stronger their belief.

Mrs Tang turned to Mei. "You're some kind of investigator, aren't you? Perhaps you can help to find Little Flower."

"That's why I'm here. Mrs Chen, please tell me what happened," Mei said.

Mrs Chen wiped her eyes with a hand. "My baby's gone. My little treasure ... We were going to buy fillings for dumplings. Little Flower loves to help in the kitchen. I was making some noodle soup for lunch. She went to play by the gate. She always played there. She had a little spinning top. We bought it together at the Temple Fair last week." Tears surged again. Mrs Chen choked. "What am I going to do? How can I live?"

"Mrs Chen, we'll find Little Flower. You must keep on believing." Mrs Tang rested her hands on Mrs Chen's shoulder.

The neighbourhood women went to get fresh towels and some water. Mr Tang slipped out of the room, which was growing dark now that the evening was deepening. No one bothered to switch on the light.

Mei left, saying she'd be back in the morning. She didn't think Mrs Chen was in a fit state to give her any useful information.

A colourless crescent moon hung in the sky. On either side of the *hutong*, courtyard gates had been shut. The low grey walls went on, empty and still. There was a thin wintry mist at the end of the alleyway. Mei imagined families gathered at their dinner tables. They would talk about Little Flower and what had happened in their neighbourhood. They would talk about people they had known, houses that had gone.

Suddenly she felt lonely. She might have come to walk their *hutong*, but she did not belong there. She was the audience observing their drama. From outside the window she watched Little Flower, her innocent eyes twinkling, her voice soft. Then she vanished. Mei could do nothing to help.

The two white lanterns from the night before still hung mockingly above the entrance to No. 19 Tofu Mill Hutong.

28

As soon as Mei got home, she went into the kitchen and took out a bag of frozen dumplings from the freezer. She emptied them into an oiled frying-pan and switched on the stove. A ring of blue flames flared. She waited for the dumplings to sizzle, then poured water into the pan. A cloud of steam soared and she put on the lid.

The telephone rang.

"I've got the information you wanted," Chao said.

Mei's heart leaped.

"First, let me tell you about Lin. He went to West City District Number Six High School, then to Qingdao University to study marine biology. He was arrested in June 1989 for taking part in the June the fourth movement. He was twenty. The record shows that he was a member of a local anti-revolutionary gang. He participated in burning army vehicles and injuring a PLA soldier near Tiananmen Square. He opposed the Party's handling of June the fourth.

The list goes on. He was sentenced to eight years of hard labour and was released last summer, after having completed his prison term.

"On to Chen Xiaolei," Chao continued. "He went to the police academy but left early in 1989. He was decorated for bravery and revolutionary resolve after the June the fourth crackdown. Three years later he went back to the academy and finished his training. He was put in charge of traffic control in West City District and commended for good leadership during the Asia Games. A year ago he was promoted to lead the team for President Li Peng's daily travel."

"He seems very young to have achieved so much," said Mei.

"Yes, he's done well for himself."

Mei wondered if Little Flower going missing had anything to do with that success.

"Are you disappointed?" asked Chao.

"No, just distracted."

"There's more," Chao said. "The records show that Chen Xiaolei was instrumental in Lin's arrest and the star witness at his trial. His name was all over the case files."

"No!" Mei couldn't believe what she was hearing. Lin's best friend had helped to arrest him, then testified against him. What a betrayal that must have seemed.

"Then," Chao spoke again, quieter than before. He sounded uncertain. "Is there any chance you'd have dinner with me on Saturday? I won't be offended if you can't."

"I'd like to."

"You would? Great. Shall we speak on Saturday morning to arrange a time? How about the Suzhou River? Of course, if you'd rather another restaurant …"

"The Suzhou River would be lovely."

"Seven o'clock? Or later?"

"Seven's perfect," said Mei. A smile curled the corners of her lips.

Then Mei smelled trouble, a strong, musky odour. It was coming from her kitchen. She said goodbye hastily and ran.

Smoke was pouring out of the frying-pan. She turned off the stove and tried to remove the lid, which burned her fingers. She dropped it and the smoke billowed into her face. She coughed, flapping her hands frantically. The dumplings had turned to charcoal. She went into the living room and opened a window. There was little traffic on the ring road below. The cold air gushed in.

What Chao had told her did not fit with her half-formed theories. She wondered if Grandpa Wu had known about Cop Chen – or anyone else, for that matter. Mrs Chen, Big Papa Liu, Mrs Tang. What part had they played?

And how had Kaili come into it?

She went to the bedroom and lay on the bed. More questions invaded her mind. What had happened to Little Flower? Where was Lin now? Gradually she drifted into sleep.

29

The telephone rang, sounding like a siren. Mei's eyes snapped open and she stumbled out of bed.

The answering-machine came on in the living room. "This is Detective Zhao. I wanted to catch you before you went out. I've got the information. Are you up?" He was shouting.

Mei picked up the receiver. "What time is it?" She peered at the darkness outside the window.

"Five o'clock."

Mei groaned. "What have you found out?"

"You'll never guess what Kaili did — I didn't believe it when I was told so I made them show me the papers. She bought a grave in the Western Mountain burial ground. What does *that* mean? Do you think she knew she was going to die?"

"I can't think before I've had some coffee," said Mei.

"Call me back at the station as soon as you can."

Mei put down the phone and went to the kitchen. She made a cup of instant coffee, poured in milk and drank it. The sky was lightening. She telephoned Detective Zhao. "What about the migrant worker? Did you get a description?"

"I've got a photograph. It's a group shot, but you can see him clearly."

"I'm coming over."

"I was about to get some breakfast from the shop by the station."

"I'll see you there."

Mei ran to the bathroom and splashed cold water on her face. She tied her long hair into a ponytail, grabbed her bag, stuffed Lin's letters to Kaili inside it, put on her coat and went out.

A symphony of light and colour was being played out on the horizon. Dawn was rising through the morning mist.

Dashanzi looked barren in the early morning. Abandoned buildings, crumbling shacks and bare trees loomed out of the dark like monsters. Mei drove along the main street. The wind picked up scraps of paper, plastic, fish bones and an empty tin, which flew across the beam of her headlights.

She left her car under a slanting electricity pole and stepped out. Straight away the icy wind stripped her of warmth. In the squalor behind the police station, shadows stirred.

The breakfast shop seemed to be the only place that was open. A large pot stood at the back, scenting the air with the sweet smell of warm soya-bean milk. The shop owner, a nimble man in his thirties, directed a pimply helper to fry *yo bing* – oil-soaked flatbread.

Detective Zhao waved when he saw her. On the table in front of him were an empty bowl and a half-eaten *yo bing* on a plate. "I've just finished, but would you like some breakfast?"

"Yes, please." Mei sat down opposite. Having burned her dinner, she was very hungry.

Detective Zhao called to the boss to bring Mei the same as he'd had.

Mei gobbled the *yo bing*, and washed them down with soya-bean milk.

"Don't eat so fast," said Detective Zhao. "You'll get stomach-ache."

"Can I see the photo?" she asked.

Detective Zhao took a couple of papers out of his pocket and gave them to her.

She studied the picture. "That's him."

"Who?"

"Come on," said Mei, jumping up. "We must go quickly."

"Where to?"

"The Drum Tower."

30

The sun, with a thousand rays, dusted a thin veil of gold on the roofs of the courtyard houses. The Drum Tower glowed above the morning mist like a floating castle, as old and indestructible as time. The city was still, yet Mei could feel its energy surging from ancient palaces and streets, sprawling slums and gleaming new high-rises.

Two neighbourhood policemen and the caretaker of the West City No. 6 High School waited for Detective Zhao and Mei outside the gate. The policemen wore their dark green winter uniform. The caretaker was a big-bellied man in his fifties with a lame leg. The two policemen shivered inside their coats. They saluted Detective Zhao. A tall skinny officer introduced himself as Team Leader. "As requested, I've posted men at every entrance."

"Good."

"What are we doing?" asked Team Leader.

"Did you not get the call from your district command?"

"I did. But the comrade didn't say —"

Detective Zhao cut him off with an impatient wave.

"Where is the caretaker's entrance?" Mei asked the caretaker.

"At the back."

"Is it locked?"

"Yes. The school has been closed for the winter holidays."

"Show us the gate," said Mei.

Detective Zhao told the two policemen to stay on guard. He and Mei followed the caretaker to the back.

A young policeman stood smoking by a small wooden gate. It was low and half hidden under a crooked tree. He threw away the stub when he saw Detective Zhao and saluted.

Detective Zhao saluted back.

The caretaker limped up to the gate and stopped abruptly. The padlock had disappeared. He gave the gate a tug but it didn't open. "It's locked from the inside," he wheezed.

The young policeman stepped forward and yanked at the gate, trying to force it open. It rattled but remain closed.

"Stop!" hissed Detective Zhao. "You're making too much noise."

Mei glanced at the gate and the wall. It was too late to go round to another entrance. The wall was not as high here as it was at the front of the school but it was still two metres. "Can you climb the tree and get over to the other side?" she asked the young policeman.

He eyed the tree, then the wall. "I think so."

Detective Zhao gave him a boost, and he was over. A minute later, Mei heard the latch and the gate swung open. "Where is the boiler room?" she asked the caretaker.

"Straight in to the left, the first annexe."

She ran.

"Tell everyone to come in at once!" Detective Zhao ordered.

The young policeman ran off. Detective Zhao followed Mei.

The back of the high school looked as if no one went there. Virgin snow lay under leafless trees. A dozen wooden planks blocked a hole in the wall. A broken wheelbarrow sagged behind a heap of bricks.

The annexe had a tarred flat roof and two doors. One led to a storage room, the other to the boiler room. Padlocks hung unused on their hooks. Mei turned the knob, but the boiler-room door had been bolted from the inside.

"Open up!" Detective Zhao shouted, kicking the door. "Police!"

Mei opened the door to the storage room and stumbled into buckets, mops and netting. She searched and at last she found an axe.

She handed it to Detective Zhao, who brought it down hard on the boiler-room door. It cracked and chips of wood flew into the air. A child screamed. Detective Zhao swung the axe again, harder. The crack widened and the bolt inside fell to the floor with a thud.

Light poured into the boiler room. Water was dripping on to the floor from two hot taps that had been wrapped in strips of cloth. There was a strong smell of wet metal. Little Flower trembled in a corner under a padded winter coat.

Mei knelt beside her and took the shivering little body into her arms. Little Flower's pigtails had come undone and her hair was a mass of tangles. Her eyes were wide with fright. Mei stroked her and whispered, "You're safe now. It's all over."

Then, her head turned and she saw him, so still and silent that he seemed to melt into the background. A rusty tin cup lay on the floor next to his feet. His gaze was empty. An eerie tremor passed through Mei.

Detective Zhao pounced, knocking him to the floor. He landed heavily, his face expressionless. When Detective Zhao clasped a pair of handcuffs on to his wrists, he simply lowered his eyes.

Mei picked up Little Flower, who was whimpering, and walked out of the boiler room. Behind them, Detective Zhao pushed the handcuffed man along. As they went out into brilliant sunshine, Little Flower hid her face in Mei's chest.

A group of policemen ran towards them, Team Leader at the front. "You've found Little Flower!" her panted. "Is he the –?"

"Yes."

Team Leader grabbed the captive by his collar. "Why?" he shouted. The man neither raised his eyes nor replied. "Speak!" screamed Team Leader, his face turning red. Suddenly he raised his foot and kicked the man.

The other policemen joined in.

"Stop!" shouted Detective Zhao. "Have you no sense of discipline?"

The prisoner lay on the ground, defenceless, bruised and bleeding.

"Who told you to beat him?" Detective Zhao stormed. "What kind of team leader are you? Take Little Flower to her mother. She's waiting."

Team Leader picked up his hat, which had fallen on the ground. Mei handed Little Flower to him. "Tell Mrs Chen that we'll come and talk to Little Flower when she's settled," she said.

Team Leader left with the child in his arms, two of his men following him.

"Get up!" Detective Zhao said hoarsely to the man on the ground.

"Let's take him into one of the classrooms and clean him up," said Mei to Detective Zhao. "As I promised, I'll explain everything"

They went into the first classroom on the ground floor and Mei closed the door.

"Sit down!" Detective Zhao pushed the man on to a chair.

"Do you mind taking off his handcuffs?" asked Mei. "He's not dangerous."

"What?"

Mei dragged over a chair and sat down. "Hello, Lin," she said.

His eyes moved behind swollen lids. Mei remembered the pictures she'd seen in Grandpa Wu's house. The man before her barely resembled the handsome young Lin.

"I'm sorry about your grandfather. You must be so sad. I

went to his wake. Many old friends and neighbours came to mourn him."

Blood seeped out of a cut on Lin's face. Mei offered him a packet of tissues, but he didn't take it. Instead he wiped off the blood with a palm.

Detective Zhao unlocked the handcuffs. Lin rubbed his wrists. His hands were dirty and chapped.

"Would you like some breakfast? You must be hungry. I'm afraid it might be your last on the outside," said Mei.

"Breakfast? But he's a killer and a kidnapper!" protested Detective Zhao.

"I didn't kill anyone," Lin said.

Detective Zhao ignored him. "I don't understand. How does Kaili's death link with the little girl?"

"It's a long story. Breakfast should help," said Mei.

Detective Zhao grunted. Outside in the playground, the three remaining policemen were playing tag. He pushed open a window. "You," he called to the youngest. "Can you get us some breakfast? Soya-bean milk and *yo bing*."

Mei fixed her eyes on those bruised lids and tried to sense the life behind them. Lin was only twenty-nine. Years ago he had risen against the wind and shouted with the recklessness and insolence only youth could afford: "Here I am. I shall triumph. Behold."

But Mei could find none of that in his eyes now. What she saw was loss. She took the paper butterfly out of her bag and laid it on the table.

"Where did you find that?" Lin asked.

"In Kaili's apartment."

Lin leaned forward and stared at her. "Are you a friend?"

"I wish I could say I was – of Kaili or you, I feel like one – but I'm a private investigator. Kaili's record company hired me to look for her when she went missing. I'm sorry everything had to end like this." Mei paused. "I wish I could have helped you. I wish someone had helped you all those years ago." Her voice shook as she thought of Tiananmen Square, the sound of tanks rolling down Changan Boulevard and the bullet whizzing past her ear. She bowed her head in admiration and respect for a fellow student who had been in the square on that fateful night.

Lin ground his teeth. The wound on his face bled again. This time he staunched it with a tissue.

Mei continued, "If my best friend had betrayed me and sent me to prison, I would have wanted revenge too. But kidnapping Little Flower? No, Lin. She's innocent."

"Innocent? Why don't you spend eight years in a *lao gai*? Then you can talk to me about innocence."

"I'm sorry."

"Sorry? I was twenty, in love and studying at university. My future lay ahead of me. Chen Xiaolei destroyed it so that he could get ahead – *shang guan fa cai*. Now he's got the brilliant career he wanted, a new car, money. He has a wife and a daughter. But look at me!" He leaped to his feet.

Detective Zhao pushed him back into his seat.

"I've lost everything and everyone I ever loved." Lin's voice cracked. "There's no innocence when one man does that to another. Fatty and I had been friends since boyhood. I told him everything. I told Mrs Tang. I trusted them. Innocent people had died that night, young people, eighteen, nineteen and twenty. They shouldn't have died. They should have been at home having dinner with their mothers, their girlfriends or boyfriends. I wanted Fatty and Mrs Tang to understand what a tragedy it had been – to see the blood and death. But they betrayed me. Mrs Tang was so convinced I was anti-revolutionary that she made sure I was at home when the police came."

"What about Big Papa Liu?"

"He does more damage with his tongue than others with a knife. But poor Grandpa, he didn't know any of this. He thought his neighbours were his friends."

Lin gazed out of the window. "This is where we used to spend time together. Every morning I came in early with Grandpa to sweep the yard and light the stoves. I grew up here and saw him get old. He never stopped working, not even when he was ill. He put me through school and supported me in everything I did. After I was sent to the *lao gai* he only continued to live so that he could see me again when I was released.

"On the night of the snowstorm, I thought I'd killed Kaili – not with my hands but it was because of me that she died. I was going mad and felt completely lost. I had nowhere else to go so I went to Grandpa. He was very ill – I so wish I'd come back earlier, but I'd been consumed by the thought of revenge and wanted everything to be in place before I saw him."

"What happened with Kaili?" Mei asked.

"I came back to Beijing a few months ago, in autumn, wanting to punish everyone. I went round the neighbourhood many times to work out what I could do. One day I saw Little Flower with Chen Xiaolei and the idea came to me. I wanted to hurt him in the same way that he had destroyed me. I would take away his most treasured love. But something unexpected happened and ruined my plans."

"You found Kaili," said Mei.

"Yes. But how do you know that?"

"I went to the Capital Gymnasium after she disappeared. There was no way out of the backstage area except the stage door, unless you went through the construction zone. That was why no one saw her leave. But whoever took her out that way must have known the construction site well. I didn't realise it was you she'd met until later."

"I travelled to Beijing with a group of migrant workers I'd met on the train," said Lin. "I joined them, renting a bed in Dashanzi. I was working on the construction site at the Capital Gymnasium when I saw posters for Kaili's concert. I hadn't seen her for nine years. She looked hardly a day older in the picture and even more beautiful.

"That night I sneaked in from the construction zone to see her. She was so surprised that she burst into tears. She said she'd been to see Grandpa and that he hadn't been well. I asked her to come with me and she did. We went to Dashanzi to one of the empty buildings. She was mine, my love, my secret. I didn't want anyone else to see her. I didn't want the police to come and take her away. We spent two days together, as if we had never stopped loving each other. We even talked about finding an apartment and starting again. But then she got restless. She said she'd made a mistake in coming with me. She said that she was hurt because her boyfriend was having an affair. She missed her apartment, her lifestyle. She said her boyfriend had got her on drugs. I told her I'd help her to come off it, but she said it was too late. She said she had changed, there wasn't any future for us, but she'd be happy to give me some money.

"We had a fight. She wanted to leave. I tried to stop her. She began to scream. I panicked. I wanted to make her stop. When I realised what I was doing, I let her go. She fell backwards down the stairs and hit her head on the sharp edge of a step. When I came down, she was dead.

"I didn't know what to do. My head was hurting – I've had a headache for years. I took her jewellery to try to make it look like robbery and fled. I didn't know where to go so I got on to a bus for the city. I wandered around in the snow. I had nowhere to go and there was no one to help me.

"When Grandpa saw me, he cried. We both did. He had grown old and frail. I could feel there was only a thread of life left in him. He had waited for me.

"I touched his face, wrapped my arms round him and lay down next to him. All I wanted was to be there and feel his love again.

"But it wasn't to be. He had waited too long and was exhausted. He died that night. I was distraught, mad with grief and hatred. If I'd had any doubt about vengeance, Grandpa's death erased it. I made paper butterflies and left them outside my enemies' houses. I wanted them to know that I would avenge the wrongs they'd done us. I'd lost the last person I loved. There was nothing left for me to fear."

"Where were you in the days after your grandfather died? What did you do?" Mei asked.

"I registered with one of the *hutong* rickshaw-tour companies. They had a lot of openings because the migrant workers were going home for the Spring Festival. I rented a small room nearby so that I could make my plans."

There was a knock on the door. It was breakfast — soya-bean milk and *yo bing*.

Detective Zhao took it and thanked the policeman. He placed it on the table and Lin devoured the food.

"Tell me about Little Flower. What happened?" Mei asked, when Lin had finished eating.

"I'd thought about taking her but didn't know how to do it. Each day I drove down Tofu Mill Hutong, sometimes with tourists in my rickshaw, sometimes alone, plotting. No one in the neighbourhood recognised me. They thought I was one of the migrant workers. I didn't dare go back to our house after I'd delivered the paper butterflies. I was afraid Fatty would be suspicious. I heard about the wake and was angry. They'd betrayed Grandpa, then pretended to mourn him.

"The next day I was back in the *hutong*. The sight of white lanterns made me dizzy. Then, as if a chance was granted to me by heaven, I saw Little Flower playing outside alone. There was no one about. I took my chance. I'd spoken to her before, so it wasn't hard to convince her to come for a ride in my rickshaw. But I knew she wouldn't sit there quietly for long, so I brought her here. Grandpa was caretaker at this school for many years. I knew it well and was pleased to find the key still hidden in a crack under the wall at the caretaker's gate. Grandpa used to put it there.

"I knew that the boiler room was never locked and would be warm at night. When Little Flower struggled and screamed, I tied her up. She fought a lot and didn't go to sleep for a long time. I planned to go out for food at daybreak."

"What did you plan to do with Little Flower?" questioned Detective Zhao.

"I hadn't thought about that."

"Kidnapping is a serious crime, especially when it affects a policeman," said Detective Zhao.

Lin lowered his head. "What punishment can I fear? I've nothing to lose and nothing to gain. This is the end. Life has no meaning. None. But I didn't kill Kaili." Lin raised his head. "You've got to believe me. It was an accident. I don't want to be condemned for something I haven't done."

"You need not worry about that," said Mei, glancing at the detective, who was sitting on a table with his long legs stretched out. Their eyes met. He agreed.

More uniformed policemen entered the schoolyard. Detective Zhao stood up. "I'm afraid this is it." He put the handcuffs back on Lin's wrists. "You'd better come with me."

31

Two days before New Year's Eve, Kaili's parents arrived in Beijing to take their daughter home. Mei met them and Manyu at the cemetery. They had already completed the paperwork and were waiting for the urn.

They were both in their fifties, but looked older. Her father, Mr Kang, was a short man with a severe but handsome face. Mrs Kang was even shorter than her husband and plump. They were wearing grey Mao jackets.

Mei introduced herself and offered her condolences. Mr Kang nodded and his wife sobbed. Mei sat down beside them on the bench. She asked whether they'd been to Beijing before.

"This is our first time," Mrs Kang told her, sniffing.

"Won't you stay for a couple of days and see the city?" Mei asked.

"We can't," Mr Kang said abruptly. "This trip has already cost us a lot of money."

"I'd be happy to pay," said Mei. "Kaili loved Beijing."

"That's what Mr Peng said. What a kind man. He said he'd tried to help our Kaili – imagine that, when he's so important. He said there would be a memorial album for her. But we must go home," said Mrs Kang.

Manyu explained that Kaili had a sixteen-year-old brother.

They were silent for a while.

"Kaili was a star. You must have been very proud of her," said Mei.

"We don't have a television and we don't listen to that kind of music," replied Mr Kang.

Mrs Kang looked at her husband timidly. More tears had formed in her eyes. She turned away her head so that he wouldn't see them.

A large group of people, led by a man carrying a black-ribboned photograph of an old lady, came into the hall. In keeping with tradition, he was weeping loudly. He was probably the dead woman's son. The group went up to the counter and were shown various urns for purchase.

"We've bought a pig for the Spring Festival," said Mrs Kang. "It's our turn to host the family dinner. Two sets of grandparents, aunts and uncles." She proceeded to tell Mei how the different parts of the pig should be cooked – the head was best boiled, which took a long time, but the ears were delicious marinated in soy sauce with garlic.

"Kang Kaili!" someone called.

Everyone was startled. Mrs Kang clutched at her husband.

"Your urn's ready!"

Mr Kang and Manyu went over to him. They came back with a small plain black box.

Mrs Kang stood up and reached out for it. Her hands shook like autumn leaves. Mr Kang handed it to her and she broke down.

He snatched it back. "Enough!" he barked at his wife. "She didn't die with honour. She fell downstairs drunk. I've told you a hundred times – the way she lived her life, something like this was sure to happen. Now let's go. We don't want to miss our train."

Mrs Kang took a last glance at the hall where plain wooden urns were displayed with ivory ones in glass cases.

Manyu and Mei took them to the station. It was pandemonium. Every Spring Festival, the government allowed migrant workers to travel without papers so that they could go home for the holiday. Thousands had camped at the station entrance. As soon as the barrier opened, they charged towards it, hauling large sacks and pushing each other.

Mei and Manyu fought their way through with Kaili's parents. Mrs Kang clasped her daughter's urn so tightly that Mei feared she might break it.

Mei wanted to buy a platform ticket so that she and Manyu could see them to their train, but they refused. They said goodbye at the barrier. Mei watched them walk away. Mr Kang's back was rigidly straight while his wife, a step behind him, was hunched.

Manyu and Mei left the station. "What a mad day," exclaimed Manyu. "And what a hypocrite! Not the mother,

I'm talking about Kaili's father. He condemned her but happily took her money."

They walked for a while without speaking.

"When is Lin's trial?" Manyu asked eventually.

"In two months."

"What are his chances?"

"He might be sentenced to death."

They drove back to the city centre together. Red lanterns shone along the wide avenues. Multi-storey office blocks were lit up and fireworks exploded, sparkling, into the sky. Drums, cymbals and trumpets echoed everywhere. The new-year celebration had begun.

Postscript

Under the blue sky and the fluffy white clouds the landscape was green. The air smelled of spring.

Mei and Gupin climbed the trail to the Western Mountain burial ground. They didn't speak much. On the same trail, in front and behind them, were families that had come out for *Qing Ming* – the Festival of the Dead. Tiny children were carried on parents' backs, and grandparents were helped along by reluctant youngsters.

Lin had been sentenced to sixteen years in prison for kidnapping Little Flower. The judge had told him that he should thank Cop Chen, for not having requested the death penalty. Mei visited Lin before he was sent to Dongbei. He asked her to look after his grandfather's grave, which Kaili had bought for him. Now Mei tided it and laid a paper-flower ring in front of the headstone, which bore Grandpa Wu's name in Mandarin and Manchu. Gupin began to burn ghost money in an aluminium washing basin. Two graves away, a woman wearing a white headband sobbed loudly "Mama!"

Mei turned. The valley below extended into vast flatlands, roads carving through them. Then came the city, an endless spread of structures and lives.

Mei wondered whether Lin would ever come back.

She reached inside her handbag and took out the paper butterfly she had found in Kaili's apartment. She raised it to her eyes and turned it gently. The golden veins caught in the sunlight. Behind the glitter, she could just make out a few landmarks – the Bell Tower, the Drum Tower, the TV tower.

Her last conversation with Lin returned to her. She had asked him what the paper butterfly meant. He had answered softly, "It is your guide in the next world. It leads you to the gate of paradise."

A light breeze rose from behind the mountains. It lifted the wings of the butterfly. Mei dropped it into the basin where the ghost money was burning. It fluttered, then the fire consumed it.